# THE SHAVING OF SHAGPAT

George Meredith

VOL.-1

**CONTENTS**

THE THWACKINGS

AND THIS IS THE STORY OF BHANAVAR THE BEAUTIFUL

# THE THWACKINGS

It was ordained that Shibli Bagarag, nephew to the renowned Baba Mustapha, chief barber to the Court of Persia, should shave Shagpat, the son of Shimpoor, the son of Shoolpi, the son of Shullum; and they had been clothiers for generations, even to the time of Shagpat, the illustrious.

Now, the story of Shibli Bagarag, and of the ball he followed, and of the subterranean kingdom he came to, and of the enchanted palace he entered, and of the sleeping king he shaved, and of the two princesses he released, and of the Afrite held in subjection by the arts of one and bottled by her, is it not known as 'twere written on the finger-nails of men and traced in their corner-robes? As the poet says:

```
Ripe with oft telling and old is the tale,
But 'tis of the sort that can never grow stale.
```

Now, things were in that condition with Shibli Bagarag, that on a certain day he was hungry and abject, and the city of Shagpat the clothier was before him; so he made toward it, deliberating as to how he should procure a meal, for he had not a dirhem in his girdle, and the remembrance of great dishes and savoury ingredients were to him as the illusion of rivers sheening on the sands to travellers gasping with thirst.

And he considered his case, crying, 'Surely this comes of wandering, and 'tis the curse of the inquiring spirit! for in Shiraz, where my craft is in favour, I should be sitting now with my uncle, Baba Mustapha, the loquacious one, cross-legged, partaking of seasoned sweet dishes, dipping my fingers in them, rejoicing my soul with scandal of the Court!'

Now, he came to a knoll of sand under a palm, from which the yellow domes and mosques of the city of Shagpat, and its black cypresses, and marble palace fronts, and shining pillars, and lofty carven arches that spanned half-circles of the hot grey sky, were plainly visible. Then gazed he awhile despondingly on the city of Shagpat, and groaned in contemplation of his evil plight, as is said by the poet:

```
The curse of sorrow is comparison!
    As the sun casteth shade, night showeth star,
We, measuring what we were by what we are,
    Behold the depth to which we are undone.
```

Wherefore he counselleth:

```
Look neither too much up, nor down at all,
But, forward stepping, strive no more to fall.
```

And the advice is excellent; but, as is again said:

> The preacher preacheth, and the hearer heareth,
> But comfort first each function requireth.

And 'wisdom to a hungry stomach is thin pottage,' saith the shrewd reader of men. Little comfort was there with Shibli Bagarag, as he looked on the city of Shagpat the clothier! He cried aloud that his evil chance had got the better of him, and rolled his body in the sand, beating his breast, and conjuring up images of the profusion of dainties and the abundance of provision in Shiraz, exclaiming, 'Well-a-way and woe's me! this it is to be selected for the diversion of him that plotteth against man.' Truly is it written:

> On different heads misfortunes come:
>   One bears them firm, another faints,
> While this one hangs them like a drum
>   Whereon to batter loud complaints.

And of the three kinds, they who bang the drum outnumber the silent ones as do the billows of the sea the ships that swim, or the grains of sand the trees that grow; a noisy multitude.

Now, he was in the pits of despondency, even as one that yieldeth without further struggle to the waves of tempest at midnight, when he was ware of one standing over him,—a woman, old, wrinkled, a very crone, with but room for the drawing of a thread between her nose and her chin; she was, as is cited of them who betray the doings of Time,

> Wrinkled at the rind, and overripe at the core,

and every part of her nodded and shook like a tree sapped by the waters, and her joints were sharp as the hind-legs of a grasshopper; she was indeed one close-wrecked upon the rocks of Time.

Now, when the old woman had scanned Shibli Bagarag, she called to him, 'O thou! what is it with thee, that thou rollest as one reft of his wits?'

He answered her, 'I bewail my condition, which is beggary, and the lack of that which filleth with pleasantness.'

So the old woman said, 'Tell me thy case.'

He answered her, 'O old woman, surely it was written at my birth that I should take ruin from the readers of planets. Now, they proclaimed that I was one day destined for great things, if I stood by my tackle, I, a barber. Know then, that I have had many offers and bribes, seductive ones, from the rich and the exalted in rank; and I heeded them not, mindful of what was foretold of me. I stood by my tackle as a warrior standeth by his arms, flourishing them. Now, when I found great things came not to me, and 'twas the continuance of sameness and satiety with Baba Mustapha, my uncle, in Shiraz,—the tongue-wagger, the endless tattler,—surely I was advised by the words of the poet to go forth in search of what was wanting, and he says:

> "Thou that dreamest an Event,
> While Circumstance is but a waste of sand,

> Arise, take up thy fortunes in thy hand,
>   And daily forward pitch thy tent."

Now, I passed from city to city, proclaiming my science, holding aloft my tackle. Wullahy! many adventures were mine, and if there's some day propitiousness in fortune, O old woman, I'll tell thee of what befell me in the kingdom of Shah Shamshureen: 'tis wondrous, a matter to draw down the lower jaw with amazement! Now, so it was, that in the eyes of one city I was honoured and in request, by reason of my calling, and I fared sumptuously, even as a great officer of state surrounded by slaves, lounging upon clouds of silk stuffs, circled by attentive ears: in another city there was no beast so base as I. Wah! I was one hunted of men and an abomination; no housing for me, nought to operate upon. I was the lean dog that lieth in wait for offal. It seemeth certain, O old woman, that a curse hath fallen on barbercraft in these days, because of the Identical, whose might I know not. Everywhere it is growing in disrepute; 'tis languishing! Nevertheless till now I have preserved my tackle, and I would descend on yonder city to exercise it, even for a livelihood, forgetting awhile great things, but that I dread men may have changed there also,—and there's no stability in them, I call Allah (whose name be praised!) to witness; so should I be a thing unsightly, subject to hateful castigation; wherefore is it that I am in that state described by the poet, when,

> "Dreading retreat, dreading advance to make,
>  Round we revolve, like to the wounded snake."

Is not my case now a piteous one, one that toucheth the tender corner in man and woman?'

When she that listened had heard him to an end, she shook her garments, crying, 'O youth, son of my uncle, be comforted! for, if it is as I think, the readers of planets were right, and thou art thus early within reach of great things—nigh grasping them.'

Then she fell to mumbling and reciting jigs of verse, quaint measures; and she pored along the sand to where a line had been drawn, and saw that the footprints of the youth were traced along it. Lo, at that sight she clapped her hands joyfully, and ran up to the youth, and peered in his face, exclaiming, 'Great things indeed! and praise thou the readers of planets, O nephew of the barber, they that sent thee searching the Event thou art to master. Wullahy! have I not half a mind to call thee already Master of the Event?'

Then she abated somewhat in her liveliness, and said to him, 'Know that the city thou seest is the city of Shagpat, the clothier, and there's no one living on the face of earth, nor a soul that requireth thy craft more than he. Go therefore thou, bold of heart, brisk, full of the sprightliness of the barber, and enter to him. Lo, thou'lt see him lolling in his shop-front to be admired of this people—marvelled at. Oh! no mistaking of Shagpat, and the mole might discern Shagpat among myriads of our kind; and enter thou to him gaily, as to perform a friendly office, one meriting thanks and gratulations, saying, "I will preserve thee the Identical!" Now he'll at first feign not to understand thee, dense of wit that he is! but mince not matters with him, perform well thy operation, and thou wilt come to great things. What say I? 'tis certain that when thou hast shaved Shagpat thou wilt have achieved the greatest of things, and be most noteworthy of thy race, thou, Shibli Bagarag, even thou! and thou wilt be Master of the Event, so named in anecdotes and histories and records, to all succeeding generations.'

At her words the breast of Shibli Bagarag took in a great wind, and he hung his head a moment to ponder them; and he thought, 'There's provokingness in the speech of this old woman, and she's one that instigateth keenly. She called me by my name! Heard I that? 'Tis a mystery!' And he thought, 'Peradventure she is a Genie, one of an ill tribe, and she's luring me to my perdition in this city! How if that be so?' And again he thought, 'It cannot be! She's probably the Genie that presided over my birth, and promised me dower of great things through the mouths of the readers of planets.'

Now, when Shibli Bagarag had so deliberated, he lifted his sight, and lo, the old woman was no longer before him! He stared, and rubbed his eyes, but she was clean gone. Then ran he to the knolls and eminences that were scattered about, to command a view, but she was nowhere visible. So he thought, "Twas a dream!' and he was composing himself to despair upon the scant herbage of one of those knolls, when as he chanced to gaze down the city below, he saw there a commotion and a crowd of people flocking one way; he thought, "Twas surely no dream? come not Genii, and go they not, in the fashion of that old woman? I'll even descend on yonder city, and try my tackle on Shagpat, inquiring for him, and if he is there, I shall know I have had to do with a potent spirit. Allah protect me!'

So, having shut together the clasps of resolve, he arose and made for the gates of the city, and entered it by the principal entrance. It was a fair city, the fairest and chief of that country; prosperous, powerful; a mart for numerous commodities, handicrafts, wares; round it a wild country and a waste of sand, ruled by the lion in his wrath, and in it the tiger, the camelopard, the antelope, and other animals. Hither, in caravans, came the people of Oolb and the people of Damascus, and the people of Vatz, and they of Bagdad, and the Ringheez, great traders, and others, trading; and there was constant flow of intercourse between them and the city of Shagpat. Now as Shibli Bagarag paced up one of the streets of the city, he beheld a multitude in procession following one that was crowned after the manner of kings, with a glittering crown, clad in the yellow girdled robes, and he sporting a fine profusion of hair, unequalled by all around him, save by one that was a little behind, shadowed by his presence. So Shibli Bagarag thought, 'Is one of this twain Shagpat? for never till now have I seen such rare growths, and 'twere indeed a bliss to slip the blade between them and those masses of darkness that hang from them.' Then he stepped before the King, and made himself prominent in his path, humbling himself; and it was as he anticipated, the King prevented his removal by the slaves that would have dragged him away, and desired a hearing as to his business, and what brought him to the city, a stranger.

Thereupon Shibli Bagarag prostrated himself and cried, 'O great King, Sovereign of the Time! surely I am one to be looked on with the eye of grace; and I am nephew to Baba Mustapha, renowned in Shiraz, a barber;—I a barber, and it is my prayer, O King of the Age, that thou take me under thy protection and the shield of thy fair will, while I perform good work in this city by operating on the unshorn.'

When he had spoken, the King made a point of his eyebrows, and exclaimed, 'Shiraz? So they hold out against Shagpat yet, aha? Shiraz! that nest of them! that reptile's nest!' Then he turned to his Vizier beside him, and said, 'What shall be done with this fellow?'

So the Vizier replied, "Twere well, O King, he be summoned to a sense of the loathsomeness of his craft by the agency of fifty stripes.'

The King said, "Tis commanded!'

Then he passed forward in his majesty, and Shibli Bagarag was ware of the power of five slaves upon him, and he was hurried at a quick pace through the streets and before the eyes of the people, even to the common receptacle of felons, and there received from each slave severally ten thwacks with a thong: 'tis certain that at every thwack the thong took an airing before it descended upon him. Then loosed they him, to wander whither he listed; and disgust was strong in him by reason of the disgrace and the severity of the administration of the blows. He strayed along the streets in wretchedness, and hunger increased on him, assailing him first as a wolf in his vitals, then as it had been a chasm yawning betwixt his trunk and his lower members. And he thought, 'I have been long in chase of great things, and the hope of attaining them is great; yet, wullahy! would I barter all for one refreshing meal, and the sense of fulness. 'Tis so, and sad is it!' And he was mindful of the poet's words,—

```
Who seeks the shadow to the substance sinneth,
And daily craving what is not, he thinneth:
    His lean ambition how shall he attain?
For with this constant foolishness he doeth,
He, waxing liker to what he pursueth,
    Himself becometh what he chased in vain!
```

And again:

```
Of honour half my fellows boast,—
    A thing that scorns and kills us:
Methinks that honours us the most
    Which nourishes and fills us.
```

So he thought he would of a surety fling far away his tackle, discard barbercraft, and be as other men, a mortal, forgotten with his generation. And he cried aloud, 'O thou old woman! thou deceiver! what halt thou obtained for me by thy deceits? and why put I faith in thee to the purchase of a thwacking? Woe's me! I would thou hadst been but a dream, thou crone! thou guileful parcel of belabouring bones!'

Now, while he lounged and strolled, and was abusing the old woman, he looked before him, and lo, one lolling in his shop-front, and people standing outside the shop, marking him with admiration and reverence, and pointing him out to each other with approving gestures. He who lolled there was indeed a miracle of hairiness, black with hair as he had been muzzled with it, and his head as it were a berry in a bush by reason of it. Then thought Shibli Bagarag, "Tis Shagpat! If the mole could swear to him, surely can I.' So he regarded the clothier, and there was naught seen on earth like the gravity of Shagpat as he lolled before those people, that failed not to assemble in groups and gaze at him. He was as a sleepy lion cased in his mane; as an owl drowsy in the daylight. Now would he close an eye, or move two fingers, but of other motion made he none, yet the people gazed at him with eagerness. Shibli Bagarag was astonished at them, thinking, 'Hair! hair! There is might in hair; but there is greater might in the barber!

Nevertheless here the barber is scorned, the grower of crops held in amazing reverence.' Then thought he, "Tis truly wondrous the crop he groweth; not even King Shamshureen, after a thousand years, sported such mighty profusion! Him I sheared: it was a high task!—why not this Shagpat?'

Now, long gazing on Shagpat awoke in Shibli Bagarag fierce desire to shear him, and it was scarce in his power to restrain himself from flying at the clothier, he saying, 'What obstacle now? what protecteth him? Nay, why not trust to the old woman? Said she not I should first essay on Shagpat? and 'twas my folly in appealing to the King that brought on me that thwacking. 'Tis well! I'll trust to her words. Wullahy! will it not lead me to great things?'

So it was, that as he thought this he continued to keep eye on Shagpat, and the hunger that was in him passed, and became a ravenous vulture that flew from him and singled forth Shagpat as prey; and there was no help for it but in he must go and state his case to Shagpat, and essay shearing him.

Now, when he was in the presence, he exclaimed, 'Peace, O vendor of apparel, unto thee and unto thine!'

Shagpat answered, 'That with thee!'

Said Shibli Bagarag, 'I have heard of thee, O thou wonder! Wullahy! I am here to render homage to that I behold.'

Shagpat answered, "Tis well!'

Then said Shibli Bagarag, 'Praise my discretion! I have even this day entered the city, and it is to thee I offer the first shave, O tangle of glory!'

At these words Shagpat darkened, saying gruffly, 'Thy jest is offensive, and it is unseasonable for staleness and lack of holiness.'

But Shibli Bagarag cried, 'No jest, O purveyor to the outward of us! but a very excellent earnest.'

Thereat the face of Shagpat was as an exceeding red berry in a bush, and he said angrily, 'Have done! no more of it! or haply my spleen will be awakened, and that of them who see with more eyes than two.'

Nevertheless Shibli Bagarag urged him, and he winked, and gesticulated, and pointed to his head, crying, 'Fall not, O man of the nicety of measure, into the trap of error; for 'tis I that am a barber, and a rarity in this city, even Shibli Bagarag of Shiraz! Know me nephew of the renowned Baba Mustapha, chief barber to the Court of Persia. Languishest thou not for my art? Lo! with three sweeps I'll give thee a clean poll, all save the Identical! and I can discern and save it; fear me not, nor distrust my skill and the cunning that is mine.'

When he had heard Shibli Bagarag to a close, the countenance of Shagpat waxed fiery, as it had been flame kindled by travellers at night in a thorny bramble-bush, and he ruffled, and heaved, and was as when dense jungle-growths are stirred violently by the near approach of a wild animal in his fury, shouting in short breaths, 'A barber! a barber! Is't so? can it be? To me? A barber! O thou, thou reptile! filthy thing! A barber! O dog! A barber? What? when I bid fair for the highest honours known? O sacrilegious wretch! monster! How? are the Afrites jealous, that they send thee to jibe me?'

Thereupon he set up a cry for his wife, and that woman rushed to him from an inner room, and fell upon Shibli Bagarag, belabouring him.

So, when she was weary of this, she said, 'O light of my eyes! O golden crop and adorable man! what hath he done to thee?'

Shagpat answered, "Tis a barber! and he hath sworn to shave me, and leave me not save shorn!'

Hardly had Shagpat spoken this, when she became limp with the hearing of it. Then Shibli Bagarag slunk from the shop; but without the crowd had increased, seeing an altercation, and as he took to his heels they followed him, and there was uproar in the streets of the city and in the air above them, as of raging Genii, he like a started quarry doubling this way and that, and at the corners of streets and open places, speeding on till there was no breath in his body, the cry still after him that he had bearded Shagpat. At last they came up with him, and belaboured him each and all; it was a storm of thwacks that fell on the back of Shibli Bagarag. When they had wearied themselves in this fashion, they took him as had he been a stray bundle or a damaged bale, and hurled him from the gates of the city into the wilderness once more.

Now, when he was alone, he staggered awhile and then flung himself to the earth, looking neither to the right nor to the left, nor above. All he could think was, 'O accursed old woman!' and this he kept repeating to himself for solace; as the poet says:

```
'Tis sure the special privilege of hate,
To curse the authors of our evil state.
```

As he was thus complaining, behold the very old woman before him! And she wheezed, and croaked, and coughed, and shook herself, and screwed her face into a pleasing pucker, and assumed womanish airs, and swayed herself, like as do the full moons of the harem when the eye of the master is upon them. Having made an end of these prettinesses, she said, in a tone of soft insinuation, 'O youth, nephew of the barber, look upon me.'

Shibli Bagarag knew her voice, and he would not look, thinking, 'Oh, what a dreadful old woman is this! just calling on her name in detestation maketh her present to us.' So the old woman, seeing him resolute to shun her, leaned to him, and put one hand to her dress, and squatted beside him, and said, 'O youth, thou hast been thwacked!'

He groaned, lifting not his face, nor saying aught. Then said she, 'Art thou truly in search of great things, O youth?'

Still he groaned, answering no syllable. And she continued, "Tis surely in sweet friendliness I ask. Art thou not a fair youth, one to entice a damsel to perfect friendliness?'

Louder yet did he groan at her words, thinking, 'A damsel, verily!' So the old woman said, 'I wot thou art angry with me; but now look up, O nephew of the barber! no time for vexation. What says the poet?—

```
"Cares the warrior for his wounds
 When the steed in battle bounds?"
```

Moreover:

```
"Let him who grasps the crown strip not for shame,
 Lest he expose what gain'd it blow and maim!"
```

So be it with thee and thy thwacking, O foolish youth! Hide it from thyself, thou silly one! What! thou hast been thwacked, and refusest the fruit of it—which is resoluteness, strength of mind, sternness in pursuit of the object!'

Then she softened her tone to persuasiveness, saying, "Twas written I should be the head of thy fortune, O Shibli Bagarag! and thou'lt be enviable among men by my aid, so look upon me, and (for I know thee famished) thou shah presently be supplied with viands and bright wines and sweetmeats, delicacies to cheer thee.'

Now, the promise of food and provision was powerful with Shibli Bagarag, and he looked up gloomily. And the old woman smiled archly at him, and wriggled in her seat like a dusty worm, and said, 'Dost thou find me charming, thou fair youth?'

He was nigh laughing in her face, but restrained himself to reply, 'Thou art that thou art!'

Said she, 'Not so, but that I shall be.' Then she said, 'O youth, pay me now a compliment!'

Shibli Bagarag was at a loss what further to say to the old woman, for his heart cursed her for her persecutions, and ridiculed her for her vanities. At last he bethought himself of the saying of the poet, truly the offspring of fine wit, where he says:

```
   Expect no flatteries from me,
       While I am empty of good things;
   I'll call thee fair, and I'll agree
       Thou boldest Love in silken strings,
When thou bast primed me from thy plenteous store!
     But, oh! till then a clod am I:
       No seed within to throw up flowers:
     All's drouthy to the fountain dry:
       To empty stomachs Nature lowers:
The lake was full where heaven look'd fair of yore!
```

So, when he had spoken that, the old woman laughed and exclaimed, 'Thou art apt! it is well said! Surely I excuse thee till that time! Now listen! 'Tis written we work together, and I know it by divination. Have I not known thee wandering, and on thy way to this city of Shagpat, where thou'lt some day sit throned? Now I propose to thee this—and 'tis an excellent proposal—that I lead thee to great things, and make thee glorious, a sitter in high seats, Master of an Event?'

Cried he, 'A proposal honourable to thee, and pleasant in the ear.'

She added, 'Provided thou marry me in sweet marriage.'

Thereat he stared on vacancy with a serious eye, and he could scarce credit her earnestness, but she repeated the same. So presently he thought, 'This old hag appeareth deep in the fountain of events, and she will be a right arm to me in the mastering of one, a torch in darkness, seeing there is wisdom in her as well as wickedness. The thwackings?—sad was their taste, but they're in the road leading to greatness, and I cannot say she put me out of that road in putting me where they were. Her age?—shall I complain of that when it is a sign she goeth shortly altogether?'

As he was thus debating he regarded the old woman stealthily, and she was in agitation, so that her joints creaked like forest branches in a wind, and the puckers of her visage moved as do billows of the sea to and fro, and the anticipations of a fair young bride are not more eager than what was visible in the old woman. Wheedlingly she looked at him, and shaped her mouth like a bird's bill to soften it; and she drew together her dress, to give herself the look of slimness, using all fascinations. He thought, ''Tis a wondrous old woman! Marriage would seem a thing of moment to her, yet is the profit with me, and I'll agree to it.' So he said, ''Tis a pact between us, O old woman!'

Now, the eyes of the old woman brightened when she heard him, and were as the eyes of a falcon that eyeth game, hungry with red fire, and she looked brisk with impatience, laughing a low laugh and saying, 'O youth, I must claim of thee, as is usual in such cases, the kiss of contract.'

So Shibli Bagarag was mindful of what is written,

```
If thou wouldst take the great leap, be ready for the little jump,
```

and he stretched out his mouth to the forehead of the old woman. When he had done so, it was as though she had been illuminated, as when light is put in the hollow of a pumpkin. Then said she, 'This is well! this is a fair beginning! Now look, for thy fortune will of a surety follow. Call me now sweet bride, and knocker at the threshold of hearts!'

So Shibli Bagarag sighed, and called her this, and he said, 'Forget not my condition, O old woman, and that I am nigh famished.'

Upon that she nodded gravely, and arose and shook her garments together, and beckoned for Shibli Bagarag to follow her; and the two passed through the gates of the city, and held on together through divers streets and thoroughfares till they came before the doors of a palace with a pillared entrance; and the old woman passed through the doors of the palace as one familiar to them, and lo! they were in a lofty court, built all of marble, and in the middle of it a fountain playing, splashing silvery. Shibli Bagarag would have halted here to breathe the cool refreshingness of the air, but the old woman would not; and she hurried on even to the opening of a spacious Hall, and in it slaves in circle round a raised seat, where sat one that was their lord, and it was the Chief Vizier of the King.

Then the old woman turned round sharply to Shibli Bagarag, and said, 'How of thy tackle, O my betrothed?'

He answered, 'The edge is keen, the hand ready.'

Then said she, ''Tis well.'

So the old woman put her two hands on the shoulders of Shibli Bagarag, saying, 'Make thy reverence to him on the raised seat; have faith in thy tackle and in me. Renounce not either, whatsoever ensueth. Be not abashed, O my bridegroom to be!'

Thereupon she thrust him in; and Shibli Bagarag was abashed, and played foolishly with his fingers, knowing not what to do. So when the Chief Vizier saw him he cried out, 'Who art thou, and what wantest thou?'

Now, the back of Shibli Bagarag tingled when he heard the Vizier's voice, and he said, 'I am, O man of exalted condition, he whom men know as Shibli Bagarag, nephew to Baba Mustapha, the renowned of Shiraz; myself barber likewise, proud of my art, prepared to exercise it.'

Then said the Chief Vizier, 'This even to our faces! Wonderful is the audacity of impudence! Know, O nephew of the barber, thou art among them that honour not thy art. Is it not written, For one thing thou shaft be crowned here, for that thing be thwacked there? So also it is written, The tongue of the insolent one is a lash and a perpetual castigation to him. And it is written, O Shibli Bagarag, that I reap honour from thee, and there is no help but that thou be made an example of.'

So the Chief Vizier uttered command, and Shibli Bagarag was ware of the power of five slaves upon him; and they seized him familiarly, and placed him in position, and made ready his clothing for the reception of fifty other thwacks with a thong, each several thwack coming down on him with a hiss, as it were a serpent, and with a smack, as it were the mouth of satisfaction; and the people assembled extolled the Chief Vizier, saying, 'Well and valiantly done, O stay of the State! and such-like to the accursed race of barbers.'

Now, when they had passed before the Chief Vizier and departed, lo! he fell to laughing violently, so that his hair was agitated and was as a sand-cloud over him, and his countenance behind it was as the sun of the desert reflected ripplingly on the waters of a bubbling spring, for it had the aspect of merriness; and the Chief Vizier exclaimed, 'O Shibli Bagarag, have I not made fair show?'

And Shibli Bagarag said, 'Excellent fair show, O mighty one!' Yet knew he not in what, but he was abject by reason of the thwacks.

So the Vizier said, 'Thou lookest lean, even as one to whom Fortune oweth a long debt. Tell me now of thy barbercraft: perchance thy gain will be great thereby?'

And Shibli Bagarag answered, 'My gain has been great, O eminent in rank, but of evil quality, and I am content not to increase it.' And he broke forth into lamentations, crying in excellent verse:—

> Why am I thus the sport of all—
> A thing Fate knocketh like a ball
> From point to point of evil chance,
> Even as the sneer of Circumstance?
> While thirsting for the highest fame,
>   I hunger like the lowest beast:
> To be the first of men I aim
>   And find myself the least.

Now, the Vizier delayed not when he heard this to have a fair supply set before Shibli Bagarag, and meats dressed in divers fashions, spiced, and coloured, and with herbs, and wines in golden goblets, and slaves in attendance. So Shibli Bagarag ate and drank, and presently his soul arose from its prostration, and he cried, 'Wullahy! the head cook of King Shamshureen could have worked no better as regards the restorative process.'

Then said the Chief Vizier, 'O Shibli Bagarag, where now is thy tackle?'

And Shibli Bagarag winked and nodded and turned his head in the manner of the knowing ones, and he recited the verse:

> 'Tis well that we are sometimes circumspect,
>   And hold ourselves in witless ways deterred:
> One thwacking made me seriously reflect;
>   A SECOND turned the cream of love to curd:
> Most surely that profession I reject
>   Before the fear of a prospective THIRD.

So the Vizier said, "Tis well, thou turnest verse neatly' And he exclaimed extemporaneously:

> If thou wouldst have thy achievement as high
>
>   As the wings of Ambition can fly:
> If thou the clear summit of hope wouldst attain,
>   And not have thy labour in vain;
> Be steadfast in that which impell'd, for the peace
>   Of earth he who leaves must have trust:
> He is safe while he soars, but when faith shall cease,
>   Desponding he drops to the dust.

Then said he, 'Fear no further thwacking, but honour and prosperity in the place of it. What says the poet?—

> "We faint, when for the fire
>   There needs one spark;

>     We droop, when our desire
>     Is near its mark."

How near to it art thou, O Shibli Bagarag! Know, then, that among this people there is great reverence for the growing of hair, and he that is hairiest is honoured most, wherefore are barbers creatures of especial abhorrence, and of a surety flourish not. And so it is that I owe my station to the esteem I profess for the cultivation of hair, and to my persecution of the clippers of it. And in this kingdom is no one that beareth such a crop as I, saving one, a clothier, an accursed one!—and may a blight fall upon him for his vanity and his affectation of solemn priestliness, and his lolling in his shop-front to be admired and marvelled at by the people. So this fellow I would disgrace and bring to scorn,—this Shagpat! for he is mine enemy, and the eye of the King my master is on him. Now I conceive thy assistance in this matter, Shibli Bagarag,—thou, a barber.'

When Shibli Bagarag heard mention of Shagpat, and the desire for vengeance in the Vizier, he was as a new man, and he smelt the sweetness of his own revenge as a vulture smelleth the carrion from afar, and he said, 'I am thy servant, thy slave, O Vizier!' Then smiled he as to his own soul, and he exclaimed, 'On my head be it!'

And it was to him as when sudden gusts of perfume from garden roses of the valley meet the traveller's nostril on the hill that overlooketh the valley, filling him with ecstasy and newness of life, delicate visions. And he cried, 'Wullahy! this is fair; this is well! I am he that was appointed to do thy work, O man in office! What says the poet?—

>     "The destined hand doth strike the fated blow:
>     Surely the arrow's fitted to the bow!"

And he says:

>     "The feathered seed for the wind delayeth,
>     The wind above the garden swayeth,
>     The garden of its burden knoweth,
>     The burden falleth, sinketh, soweth."'

So the Vizier chuckled and nodded, saying, 'Right, right! aptly spoken, O youth of favour! 'Tis even so, and there is wisdom in what is written:

>     "Chance is a poor knave;
>       Its own sad slave;
>     Two meet that were to meet:
>       Life 's no cheat."'

Upon that he cried, 'First let us have with us the Eclipser of Reason, and take counsel with her, as is my custom.'

Now, the Vizier made signal to a slave in attendance, and the slave departed from the Hall, and the Vizier led Shibli Bagarag into a closer chamber, which had a smooth floor of inlaid silver and silken hangings, the windows looking forth on the gardens of the palace and its fountains and cool recesses of shade and temperate sweetness. While they sat there conversing in this metre and that, measuring quotations, lo! the old woman, the affianced of Shibli Bagarag—and she sumptuously arrayed, in perfect queenliness, her head bound in a circlet of gems and gold, her figure lustrous with a full robe of flowing crimson silk; and she wore slippers embroidered with golden traceries, and round her waist a girdle flashing with jewels, so that to look on she was as a long falling water in the last bright slant of the sun. Her hair hung disarranged, and spread in a scattered fashion off her shoulders; and she was younger by many moons, her brow smooth where Shibli Bagarag had given the kiss of contract, her hand soft and white where he had taken it. Shibli Bagarag was smitten with astonishment at sight of her, and he thought, 'Surely the aspect of this old woman would realise the story of Bhanavar the Beautiful; and it is a story marvellous to think of; yet how great is the likeness between Bhanavar and this old woman that groweth younger!'

And he thought again, 'What if the story of Bhanavar be a true one; this old woman such as she—no other?'

So, while he considered her, the Vizier exclaimed, 'Is she not fair—my daughter?'

And the youth answered, 'She is, O Vizier, that she is!'

But the Vizier cried, 'Nay, by Allah! she is that she will be.' And the Vizier said, ''Tis she that is my daughter; tell me thy thought of her, as thou thinkest it.'

And Shibli Bagarag replied, 'O Vizier, my thought of her is, she seemeth indeed as Bhanavar the Beautiful—no other.'

Then the Vizier and the Eclipser of Reason exclaimed together, 'How of Bhanavar and her story, O youth? We listen!'

So Shibli Bagarag leaned slightly on a cushion of a couch, and narrated as followeth.

# AND THIS IS THE STORY OF BHANAVAR THE BEAUTIFUL

Know that at the foot of a lofty mountain of the Caucasus there lieth a deep blue lake; near to this lake a nest of serpents, wise and ancient. Now, it was the habit of a damsel to pass by the lake early at morn, on her way from the tents of her tribe to the pastures of the flocks. As she pressed the white arch of her feet on the soft green-mossed grasses by the shore of the lake she would let loose her hair, looking over into the water, and bind the braid again round her temples and behind her ears, as it had been in a lucent mirror: so doing she would laugh. Her laughter was like the falls of water at moonrise; her loveliness like the very moonrise; and she was stately as a palm-tree standing before the moon.

This was Bhanavar the Beautiful.

Now, the damsel was betrothed to the son of a neighbouring Emir, a youth comely, well-fashioned, skilled with the bow, apt in all exercises; one that sat his mare firm as the trained falcon that fixeth on the plunging bull of the plains; fair and terrible in combat as the lightning that strideth the rolling storm; and it is sung by the poet:

```
When on his desert mare I see
    My prince of men,
    I think him then
As high above humanity
As he shines radiant over me.

Lo! like a torrent he doth bound,
    Breasting the shock
    From rock to rock:
A pillar of storm, he shakes the ground,

His turban on his temples wound.

Match me for worth to be adored
    A youth like him
    In heart and limb!
Swift as his anger is his sword;
Softer than woman his true word.
```

Now, the love of this youth for the damsel Bhanavar was a consuming passion, and the father of the damsel and the father of the youth looked fairly on the prospect of their union, which was near, and was plighted as the union of the two tribes. So they met, and there was no voice against their meeting, and all the love that was in them they were free to pour forth far from the hearing of men, even where they would. Before the rising of the sun, and ere his setting, the youth rode swiftly from the green tents of the Emir his father, to waylay her by the waters of the lake; and Bhanavar was there, bending over the lake, her image in the lake glowing like the fair fulness of the moon; and the youth leaned to her from his steed, and sang to her verses of her great loveliness ere she was wistful of him. Then she turned to him, and laughed lightly a welcome of sweetness, and shook the falls of her hair across the blushes of her face and her bosom; and he folded her to him, and those two would fondle together in the fashion of the betrothed ones (the blessing of Allah be on them all!), gazing on each other till their eyes swam with tears, and they were nigh swooning with the fulness of their bliss. Surely 'twas an innocent and tender dalliance, and their prattle was that of lovers till the time of parting, he showing her how she looked best—she him; and they were forgetful of all else that is, in their sweet interchange of flatteries; and the world was a wilderness to them both when the youth parted with Bhanavar by the brook which bounded the tents of her tribe.

It was on a night when they were so together, the damsel leaning on his arm, her eyes toward the lake, and lo! what seemed the reflection of a large star in the water; and there was darkness in the sky above it, thick clouds, and no sight of the heavens; so she held her face to him sideways and said, 'What meaneth this, O my betrothed? for there is reflected in yonder lake a light as of a star, and there is no star visible this night.'

The youth trembled as one in trouble of spirit, and exclaimed, 'Look not on it, O my soul! It is of evil omen.'

But Bhanavar kept her gaze constantly on the light, and the light increased in lustre; and the light became, from a pale sad splendour, dazzling in its brilliancy. Listening, they heard presently a gurgling noise as of one deeply drinking. Then the youth sighed a heavy sigh and said, 'This is the Serpent of the Lake drinking of its waters, as is her wont once every moon, and whoso heareth her drink by the sheening of that light is under a destiny dark and imminent; so know I my days are numbered, and it was foretold of me, this!' Now the youth sought to dissuade Bhanavar from gazing on the light, and he flung his whole body before her eyes, and clasped her head upon his breast, and clung about her, caressing her; yet she slipped from him, and she cried, 'Tell me of this serpent, and of this light.'

So he said, 'Seek not to hear of it, O my betrothed!'

Then she gazed at the light a moment more intently, and turned her fair shape toward him, and put up her long white fingers to his chin, and smoothed him with their softness, whispering, 'Tell me of it, my life!'

And so it was that her winningness melted him, and he said, 'Bhanavar! the serpent is the Serpent of the Lake; old, wise, powerful; of the brood of the sacred mountain, that lifteth by day a peak of gold, and by night a point of solitary silver. In her head, upon her forehead, between her eyes, there is a Jewel, and it is this light.'

Then she said, 'How came the Jewel there, in such a place?'

He answered, ''Tis the growth of one thousand years in the head of the serpent.'

She cried, 'Surely precious?'

He answered, 'Beyond price!'

As he spake the tears streamed from him, and he was shaken with grief, but she noted nought of this, and watched the wonder of the light, and its increasing, and quivering, and lengthening; and the light was as an arrow of beams and as a globe of radiance. Desire for the Jewel waxed in her, and she had no sight but for it alone, crying, ''Tis a Jewel exceeding in preciousness all jewels that are, and for the possessing it would I forfeit all that is.'

So he said sorrowfully, 'Our love, O Bhanavar? and our hopes of espousal?'

But she cried, 'No question of that! Prove now thy passion for me, O warrior! and win for me that Jewel.'

Then he pleaded with her, and exclaimed, 'Urge not this! The winning of the Jewel is worth my life; and my life, O Bhanavar—surely its breath is but the love of thee.'

So she said, 'Thou fearest a risk?'

And he replied, 'Little fear I; my life is thine to cast away. This Jewel it is evil to have, and evil followeth the soul that hath it.'

Upon that she cried, 'A trick to cheat me of the Jewel! thy love is wanting at the proof.'

And she taunted the youth her betrothed, and turned from him, and hardened at his tenderness, and made her sweet shape as a thorn to his caressing, and his heart was charged with anguish for her. So at the last, when he had wept a space in silence, he cried, 'Thou hast willed it; the Jewel shall be thine, O my soul!'

Then said he, 'Thou hast willed it, O Bhanavar! and my life is as a grain of sand weighed against thy wishes; Allah is my witness! Meet me therefore here, O my beloved, at the end of one quarter-moon, even beneath the shadow of this palm-tree, by the lake, and at this hour, and I will deliver into thy hands the Jewel. So farewell! Wind me once about with thine arms, that I may take comfort from thee.'

When their kiss was over the youth led her silently to the brook of their parting—the clear, cold, bubbling brook—and passed from her sight; and the damsel was exulting, and leapt and made circles in her glee, and she danced and rioted and sang, and clapped her hands, crying, 'If I am now Bhanavar the Beautiful how shall I be when that Jewel is upon me, the bright light which beameth in the darkness, and needeth to light it no other light? Surely there will be envy among the maidens and the widows, and my name and the odour of my beauty will travel to the courts of far kings.'

So was she jubilant; and her sisters that met her marvelled at her and the deep glow that was upon her, even as the glow of the Great Desert when the sun has fallen; and they said among themselves, 'She is covered all over with the blush of one that is a bride, and the bridegroom's kiss yet burneth upon Bhanavar!'

So they undressed her and she lay among them, and was all night even as a bursting rose in a vase filled with drooping lilies; and one of the maidens that put her hand on the left breast of Bhanavar felt it full, and the heart beneath it panting and beating swifter than the ground is struck by hooves of the chosen steed sent by the Chieftain to the city of his people with news of victory and the summons for rejoicing.

Now, the nights and the days of Bhanavar were even as this night, and she was as an unquiet soul till the appointed time for the meeting with her lover had come. Then when the sun was lighting with slant beam the green grass slope by the blue brook before her, Bhanavar arrayed herself and went forth gaily, as a martial queen to certain conquest; and of all the flowers that nodded to the setting,—yea, the crimson, purple, pure white, streaked-yellow, azure, and saffron, there was no flower fairer in its hues than Bhanavar, nor bird of the heavens freer in its glittering plumage, nor shape of loveliness such as hers. Truly, when she had taken her place under the palm by the waters of the lake, that was no exaggeration of the poet, where he says:

> Snows of the mountain-peaks were mirror'd there
>   Beneath her feet, not whiter than they were;
> Not rosier in the white, that falling flush
>   Broad on the wave, than in her cheek the blush.

And again:

> She draws the heavens down to her,
>   So rare she is, so fair she is;
> They flutter with a crown to her,
>   And lighten only where she is.

And he exclaims, in verse that applieth to her:

> Exquisite slenderness!
>  Sleek little antelope!
>  Serpent of sweetness!
>   Eagle that soaringly
>   Wins me adoringly!
>  Teach me thy fleetness,
> Vision of loveliness;
> Turn to my tenderness!

Now, when the sun was lost to earth, and all was darkness, Bhanavar fixed her eyes upon an opening arch of foliage in the glade through which the youth her lover should come to her, and clasped both hands across her bosom, so shaken was she with eager longing and expectation. In her hunger for his approach, she would at whiles pluck up the herbage about her by the roots, and toss handfuls this way and that, chiding the peaceful song of the nightbird in the leaves above her head; and she was sinking with fretfulness, when lo! from the opening arch of the glade a sudden light, and Bhanavar knew it for the Jewel in the fingers of her betrothed, by the strength of its effulgence. Then she called to him joyfully a cry of welcome, and quickened his coming with her calls, and the youth alighted from his mare and left it to pasture, and advanced to her, holding aloft the Jewel. And the Jewel was of great size and purity, round, and all-luminous, throwing rays and beams everywhere about it, a miracle to behold,—the light in it shining, and as the very life of the blood, a sweet crimson, a ruby, a softer rose, an amethyst of tender hues: it was a full globe of splendours, showing like a very kingdom of the Blest; and blessed was the eye beholding it! So when he was within reach of her arm, the damsel sprang to him and caught from his hand the Jewel, and held it before her eyes, and danced with it, and pressed it on her bosom, and was as a creature giddy with great joy in possessing it. And she put the Jewel in her bosom, and looked on the youth to thank him for the Jewel with all her beauty; for the passion of a mighty pride in him who had won for her the Jewel exalted Bhanavar, and she said sweetly, 'Now hast thou proved to me thy love of me, and I am thine, O my betrothed,—wholly thine. Kiss me, then, and cease not kissing me, for bliss is in me.'

But the youth eyed her sorrowfully, even as one that hath great yearning, and no power to move or speak.

So she said again, in the low melody of deep love-tones, 'Kiss me, O my lover! for I desire thy kiss.'

Still he spake not, and was as a pillar of stone.

And she started, and cried, 'Thou art whole? without a hurt?' Then sought she to coax him to her with all the softness of her half-closed eyes and budded lips, saying, "Twas an idle fear! and I have thee, and thou art mine, and I am thine; so speak to me, my lover! for there is no music like the music of thy voice, and the absence of it is the absence of all sweetness, and there is no pleasure in life without it.'

So the tenderness of her fondling melted the silence in him, and presently his tongue was loosed, and he breathed in pain of spirit, and his words were the words of the proverb:

```
He that fighteth with poison is no match for the prick of a thorn.
```

And he said, 'Surely, O Bhanavar, my love for thee surpasseth what is told of others that have loved before us, and I count no loss a loss that is for thy sake.' And he sighed, and sang:

```
Sadder than is the moon's lost light,
  Lost ere the kindling of dawn,
  To travellers journeying on,

The shutting of thy fair face from my sight.
  Might I look on thee in death,
  With bliss I would yield my breath.

Oh! what warrior dies
With heaven in his eyes?
O Bhanavar! too rich a prize!
  The life of my nostrils art thou,
  The balm-dew on my brow;

Thou art the perfume I meet as I speed o'er the plains,
The strength of my arms, the blood of my veins.
```

Then said he, 'I make nothing matter of complaint, Allah witnesseth! not even the long parting from her I love. What will be, will be: so was it written! 'Tis but a scratch, O my soul! yet am I of the dead and them that are passed away. 'Tis hard; but I smile in the face of bitterness.'

Now, at his words the damsel clutched him with both her hands, and the blood went from her, and she was as a block of white marble, even as one of those we meet in the desert, leaning together, marking the wrath of the All-powerful on forgotten cities. And the tongue of the damsel was dry, and she was without speech, gazing at him with wide-open eyes, like one in trance. Then she started as a dreamer wakeneth, and flung herself quickly on the breast of the youth, and put up the sleeve from his arm, and beheld by the beams of the quarter-crescent that had risen through the leaves, a small bite on the arm of the youth her betrothed, spotted with seven spots of blood in a crescent; so she knew that the poison of the serpent had entered by that bite; and she loosened herself to the violence of her anguish, shrieking the shrieks of despair, so that the voice of her lamentation was multiplied about and made many voices in the night. Her spirit returned not to her till the crescent of the moon was yellow to its fall; and lo! the youth was sighing heavy sighs and leaning to the ground on one elbow, and she flung herself by him on the ground, seeking for herbs that were antidotes to the poison of the serpent, grovelling among the grasses and strewn leaves of the wood, peering at them tearfully by the pale beams, and startling the insects as she moved. When she had gathered some, she pressed them and bruised them, and laid them along his lips, that were white as the ball of an eye; and she made him drink drops of the juices of the herbs, wailing and swaying her body across him, as one that seeketh vainly to give brightness again to the flames of a dying fire. But now his time was drawing nigh, and he was weak, and took her hand in his and gazed on her face, sighing, and said, 'There is nothing shall keep me by thee now, O my betrothed, my beautiful! Weep not, for it is the doing of fate, and not thy doing. So ere I go, and the grave-cloth separates thy heart from my heart, listen to me. Lo, that Jewel! it is the giver of years and of powers, and of loveliness beyond mortal, yet the wearing of it availeth not in the pursuit of happiness. Now art thou Queen over the serpents of this lake: it was the Queen-serpent I slew, and her vengeance is on me here. Now art thou mighty, O Bhanavar! and look to do well by thy tribe, and that from which I spring, recompensing my father for his loss, pouring ointment on his affliction, for great is the grief of the old man, and he loveth me, and is childless.'

Then the youth fell back and was still; and Bhanavar put her ear to his mouth, and heard what seemed an inner voice murmuring in him, and it was of his infancy and his boyhood, and of his father the Emir's first gift to him, his horse Zoora, in old times. Presently the youth revived somewhat, and looked upon her; but his sight was glazed with a film, and she sang her name to him ere he knew her, and the sad sweetness of her name filled his soul, and he replied to her with it weakly, like a far echo that groweth fainter, 'Bhanavar! Bhanavar! Bhanavar!' Then a change came over him, and the pain of the poison and the passion of the death-throe, and he was wistful of her no more; but she lay by him, embracing him, and in the last violence of his anguish he hugged her to his breast. Then it was over, and he sank. And the twain were as a great wave heaving upon the shore; lo, part is wasted where it falleth; part draweth back into the waters. So was it!

Now the chill of dawn breathed blue on the lake and was astir among the dewy leaves of the wood, when Bhanavar arose from the body of the youth, and as she rose she saw that his mare Zoora, his father's first gift, was snuffing at the ear of her dead master, and pawing him. At that sight the tears poured from her eyelids, and she sobbed out to the mare, 'O Zoora! never mare bore nobler burden on her back than thou in Zurvan my betrothed. Zoora! thou weepest, for death is first known to thee in the dearest thing that was thine; as to me, in the dearest that was mine! And O Zoora, steed of Zurvan my betrothed, there's no loveliness for us in life, for the loveliest is gone; and let us die, Zoora, mare of Zurvan my betrothed, for what is dying to us, O Zoora, who cherish beyond all that which death has taken?'

So spake she to Zoora the mare, kissing her, and running her fingers through the long white mane of the mare. Then she stooped to the body of her betrothed, and toiled with it to lift it across the crimson saddle-cloth that was on the back of Zoora; and the mare knelt to her, that she might lay on her back the body of Zurvan; when that was done, Bhanavar paced beside Zoora the mare, weeping and caressing her, reminding her of the deeds of Zurvan, and the battles she had borne him to, and his greatness and his gentleness. And the mare went without leading. It was broad light when they had passed the glade and the covert of the wood. Before them, between great mountains, glimmered a space of rolling grass fed to deep greenness by many brooks. The shadow of a mountain was over it, and one slant of the rising sun, down a glade of the mountain, touched the green tent of the Emir, where it stood a little apart from the others of his tribe. Goats and asses of the tribe were pasturing in the quiet, but save them nothing moved among the tents, and it was deep peacefulness. Bhanavar led Zoora slowly before the tent of the Emir, and disburdened Zoora of the helpless weight, and spread the long fair limbs of the youth lengthwise across the threshold of the Emir's tent, sitting away from it with clasped hands, regarding it. Ere long the Emir came forth, and his foot was on the body of his son, and he knew death on the chin and the eyes of Zurvan, his sole son. Now the Emir was old, and with the shock of that sight the world darkened before him, and he gave forth a groan and stumbled over the sunken breast of Zurvan, and stretched over him as one without life. When Bhanavar saw that old man stretched over the body of his son, she sickened, and her ear was filled with the wailings of grief that would arise, and she stood up and stole away from the habitations of the tribe, stricken with her guilt, and wandered beyond the mountains, knowing not whither she went, looking on no living thing, for the sight of a thing that moved was hateful to her, and all sounds were sounds of lamentation for a great loss.

Now, she had wandered on alone two days and two nights, and nigh morn she was seized with a swoon of weariness, and fell forward with her face to the earth, and lay there prostrate, even as one that is adoring the shrine; and it was on the sands of the desert she was lying. It chanced that the Chieftain of a desert tribe passed at midday by the spot, and seeing the figure of a damsel unshaded' by any shade of tree or herb or tent-covering, and prostrate on the sands, he reined his steed and leaned forward to her, and called to her. Then as she answered nothing he dismounted, and thrust his arm softly beneath her and lifted her gently; and her swoon had the whiteness of death, so that he thought her dead verily, and the marvel of her great loveliness in death smote the heart on his ribs as with a blow, and the powers of life went from him a moment as he looked on her and the long dark wet lashes that clung to her colourless face, as at night in groves where the betrothed ones wander, the slender leaves of the acacia spread darkly over the full moon. And he cried, "Tis a loveliness that maketh the soul yearn to the cold bosom of death, so lovely, exceeding all that liveth, is she!'

After he had contemplated her longwhile, he snatched his sight from her, and swung her swiftly on the back of his mare, and leaned her on one arm, and sped westward over the sands of the desert, halting not till he was in the hum of many tents, and the sun of that day hung a red half-circle across the sand. He alighted before the tent of his mother, and sent women in to her. When his mother came forth to the greetings of her son, he said no word, but pointed to the damsel where he had leaned her at the threshold of her tent. His mother kissed him on the forehead, and turned her shoulder to peer upon the damsel. But when she had close view of Bhanavar, she spat, and scattered her hair, and stamped, and cried aloud, 'Away with her! this slut of darkness! there's poison on her very skirts, and evil in the look of her.'

Then said he, 'O Rukrooth, my mother! art thou lost to charity and the uses of kindliness and the laws of hospitality, that thou talkest this of the damsel, a stranger? Take her now in, and if she be past help, as I fear; be it thy care to give her decent burial; and if she live, O my mother, tend her for the love of thy son, and for the love of him be gentle with her.'

While he spake, Rukrooth his mother knelt over the damsel, as a cat that sniffeth the suspected dish; and she flashed her eyes back on him, exclaiming scornfully, 'So art thou befooled, and the poison is already in thee! But I will not have her, O my son! and thou, Ruark, my son, neither shalt thou have her. What! will I not die to save thee from a harm? Surely thy frown is little to me, my son, if I save thee from a harm; and the damsel here is—I shudder to think what; but never lay shadow across my threshold dark as this!'

Now, Ruark gazed upon his mother, and upon Bhanavar, and the face of Bhanavar was as a babe in sleep, and his soul melted to the parted sweetness of her soft little curved red lips and her closed eyelids, and her innocent open hands, where she lay at the threshold of the tent, unconscious of hardness and the sayings of the unjust. So he cried fiercely, 'No paltering, O Rukrooth, my mother: and if not to thy tent, then to mine!'

When she heard him say that in the voice of his anger, Rukrooth fixed her eyes on him sorrowfully, and sighed, and went up to him and drew his head once against her heart, and retreated into the tent, bidding the women that were there bring in the body of the damsel.

It was the morning of another day when Bhanavar awoke; and she awoke in a dream of Zoora, the mare of Zurvan her betrothed, that was dead, and the name of Zoora was on her tongue as she started up. She was on a couch of silk and leopard-skins; at her feet a fair young girl with a fan of pheasant feathers. She stared at the hangings of the tent, which were richer than those of her own tribe; the cloths, and the cushions, and the embroideries; and the strangeness of all was pain to her, she knew not why. Then wept she bitterly, and with her tears the memory of what had been came back to her, and she opened her arms to take into them the little girl that fanned her, that she might love something and be beloved awhile; and the child sobbed with her. After a time Bhanavar said, 'Where am I, and amongst whom, my child, my sister?'

And the child answered her, 'Surely in the tent of the mother of Ruark, the chief, even chief of the Beni-Asser, and he found thee in the desert, nigh dead. 'Tis so; and this morning will Ruark be gone to meet the challenge of Ebn Asrac, and they will fight at the foot of the Snow Mountains, and the shadow of yonder date-palm will be over our tent here at the hour they fight, and I shall sing for Ruark, and kneel here in the darkness of the shadow.'

While the child was speaking there entered to them a tall aged woman, with one swathe of a turban across her long level brows; and she had hard black eyes, and close lips and a square chin; and it was the mother of Ruark. She strode forward toward Bhanavar to greet her, and folded her legs before the damsel. Presently she said, 'Tell me thy story, and of thy coming into the hands of Ruark my son.'

Bhanavar shuddered. So Rukrooth dismissed the little maiden from the chamber of the tent, and laid her left hand on one arm of Bhanavar, and said, 'I would know whence comest thou, that we may deal well by thee and thy people that have lost thee.'

The touch of a hand was as the touch of a corpse to Bhanavar, and the damsel was constrained to speak by a power she knew not of, and she told all to Rukrooth of what had been, the great misery, and the wickedness that was hers. Then Ruark's mother took hold of Bhanavar a strong grasp, and eyed her long, piteously, and with reproach, and rocked forward and back, and kept rocking to and fro, crying at intervals, 'O Ruark! my son! my son! this feared I, and thou art not the first! and I saw it, I saw it! Well-away! why came she in thy way, why, Ruark, my son, my fire-eye? Canst thou be saved by me, fated that thou art, thou fair-face? And wilt thou be saved by me, my son, ere thy story be told in tears as this one, that is as thine to me? And thou wilt seize a jewel, Ruark, O thou soul of wrath, my son, my dazzling Chief, and seize it to wear it, and think it bliss, this lovely jewel; but 'tis an anguish endless and for ever, my son! Woe's me! an anguish is she without end.'

Rukrooth continued moaning, and the thought that was in the mother of Ruark struck Bhanavar like a light in the land of despair that darkly illumineth the dreaded gulfs and abysses of the land, and she knew herself black in evil; and the scourge of her guilt was upon her, and she cursed herself before Rukrooth, and fawned before her, abasing her body. So Rukrooth was drawn to the damsel by the violence of her self-accusing and her abandonment to grief, and lifted her, and comforted her, and after awhile they had gentle speech together, and the two women opened their hearts and wept. Then it was agreed between them that Bhanavar should depart from the encampment of the tribe before the return of Ruark, and seek shelter among her own people again, and aid them and the tribe of Zurvan, her betrothed, by the might of the Jewel which was hers, fulfilling the desire of Zurvan. The mind of the damsel was lowly, and her soul yearned for the blessing of Rukrooth.

Darkness hung over the tent from the shadow of the date-palm when Bhanavar departed, and the blessing of Rukrooth was on her head. She went forth fairly mounted on a fresh steed; beside her two warriors of them that were left to guard the encampment of the tribe of Ruark in his absence; and Rukrooth watched at the threshold of her tent for the coming of Ruark.

When it was middle night, and the splendour of the moon was beaming on the edge of the desert, Bhanavar alighted to rest by the twigs of a tamarisk that stood singly on the sands. The two warriors tied the fetlocks of their steeds, and spread shawls for her, and watched over her while she slept. And the damsel dreamed, and the roaring of the lion was hoarse in her dream, and it was to her as were she the red whirlwind of the desert before whom all bowed in terror, the Arab, the wild horsemen, and the caravans of pilgrimage; and none could stay her, neither could she stay herself, for the curse of Allah was on men by reason of her guilt; and she went swinging great folds of darkness across kingdoms and empires of earth where joy was and peace of spirit; and in her track amazement and calamity, and the whitened bones of noble youths, valorous chieftains. In that horror of her dream she stood up suddenly, and thrust forth her hands as to avert an evil, and advanced a step; and with the act her dream was cloven and she awoke, and lo! it was sunrise; and where had been two warriors of the Beni-Asser, were now five, and besides her own steed five others, one the steed of Ruark, and Ruark with them that watched over her: pale was the visage of the Chief. Ruark eyed Bhanavar, and signalled to his followers, and they, when they had lifted the damsel to her steed and placed her in their front, mounted likewise, and flourished their lances with cries, and jerked their heels to the flanks of their steeds, and stretched forward till their beards were mixed with the tossing manes, and the dust rose after them crimson in the sun. So they coursed away, speeding behind their Chief and Bhanavar; sweet were the desert herbs under their crushing hooves! Ere the shadow of the acacia measured less than its height they came upon a spring of silver water, and Ruark leaped from his steed, and Bhanavar from hers, and they performed their ablutions by that spring, and ate and drank, and watered their steeds. While they were there Bhanavar lifted her eyes to Ruark, and said, 'Whither takest thou me, O my Chief?'

His brow was stern, and he answered, 'Surely to the dwelling of thy tribe.'

Then she wept, and pulled her veil close, murmuring, "Tis well!'

They spake no further, and pursued their journey toward the mountains and across the desert that was as a sea asleep in the blazing heat, and the sun till his setting threw no shade upon the sands bigger than what was broad above them. By the beams of the growing moon they entered the first gorge of the mountains. Here they relaxed the swiftness of their pace, picking their way over broken rocks and stunted shrubs, and the mesh of spotted creeping plants; all around them in shadow a freshness of noisy rivulets and cool scents of flowers, asphodel and rose blooming in plots from the crevices of the crags. These, as the troop advanced, wound and widened, gradually receding, and their summits, which were silver in the moonlight, took in the distance a robe of purple, and the sides of the mountains were rounded away in purple beyond a space of emerald pasture. Now, Ruark beheld the heaviness of Bhanavar, and that she drooped in her seat, and he halted her by a cave at the foot of the mountains, browed with white broom. Before it, over grass and cresses, ran a rill, a branch from others, larger ones, that went hurrying from the heights to feed the meadows below, and Bhanavar dipped her hand in the rill, and thought, 'I am no more as thou, rill of the mountain, but a desert thing! Thy way is forward, thy end before thee; but I go this way and that; my end is dark to me; not a life is mine that will have its close kissing the cold cheeks of the saffron-crocus. Cold art thou, and I—flames! They that lean to thee are refreshed, they that touch me perish.' Then she looked forth on the stars that were above the purple heights, and the blushes of inner heaven that streamed up the sky, and a fear of meeting the eyes of her kindred possessed her, and she cried out to Ruark, 'O Chief of the Beni-Asser, must this be? and is there no help for it, but that I return among them that look on me basely?'

Ruark stooped to her and said, 'Tell me thy name.'

She answered, 'Bhanavar is my name with that people.'

And he whispered, 'Surely when they speak of thee they say not Bhanavar solely, but Bhanavar the Beautiful?'

She started and sought the eye of the Chief, and it was fixed on her face in a softened light, as if his soul had said that thing. Then she sighed, and exclaimed, 'Unhappy are the beautiful! born to misery! Allah dressed them in his grace and favour for their certain wretchedness! Lo, their countenances are as the sun, their existence as the desert; barren are they in fruits and waters, a snare to themselves and to others!'

Now, the Chief leaned to her yet nearer, saying, 'Show me the Jewel.'

Bhanavar caught up her hands and clenched them, and she cried bitterly, "'Tis known to thee! She told thee, and there be none that know it not!'

Arising, she thrust her hand into her bosom, and held forth the Jewel in the palm of her white hand. When Ruark beheld the marvel of the Jewel, and the redness moving in it as of a panting heart, and the flashing eye of fire that it was, and all its glory, he cried, 'It was indeed a Jewel for queens to covet from the Serpent, and a prize the noblest might risk all to win as a gift for thee.'

Then she said, 'Thy voice is friendly with me, O Ruark! and thou scornest not the creature that I am. Counsel me as to my dealing with the Jewel.'

Surely the eyes of the Chief met the eyes of Bhanavar as when the brightest stars of midnight are doubled in a clear dark lake, and he sang in measured music:

```
    'Shall I counsel the moon in her ascending?
Stay under that tall palm-tree through the night;
    Rest on the mountain-slope
    By the couching antelope,
O thou enthroned supremacy of light!
  And for ever the lustre thou art lending,
Lean on the fair long brook that leaps and leaps,—
    Silvery leaps and falls.
    Hang by the mountain walls,
Moon! and arise no more to crown the steeps,
  For a danger and dolour is thy wending!
```

And, O Bhanavar, Bhanavar the Beautiful! shall I counsel thee, moon of loveliness,—bright, full, perfect moon!—counsel thee not to ascend and be seen and worshipped of men, sitting above them in majesty, thou that art thyself the Jewel beyond price? Wah! What if thou cast it from thee?—thy beauty remaineth!'

And Bhanavar smote her palms in the moonlight, and exclaimed, 'How then shall I escape this in me, which is a curse to them that approach me?'

And he replied:

```
    Long we the less for the pearl of the sea
    Because in its depths there 's the death we flee?
    Long we the less, the less, woe's me!
    Because thou art deathly,—the less for thee?
```

She sang aloud among the rocks and the caves and the illumined waters:

```
    Destiny! Destiny! why am I so dark?
      I that have beauty and love to be fair.
    Destiny! Destiny! am I but a spark
      Track'd under heaven in flames and despair?
    Destiny! Destiny! why am I desired
      Thus like a poisonous fruit, deadly sweet?
    Destiny! Destiny! lo, my soul is tired,
```

> Make me thy plaything no more, I entreat!

Ruark laughed low, and said, 'What is this dread of Rukrooth my mother which weigheth on thee but silliness! For she saw thee willing to do well by her; and thou with thy Jewel, O Bhanavar, do thou but well by thyself, and there will be no woman such as thou in power and excellence of endowments, as there is nowhere one such as thou in beauty.' Then he sighed to her, 'Dare I look up to thee, O my Queen of Serpents?' And he breathed as one that is losing breath, and the words came from him, 'My soul is thine!'

When she heard him say this, great trouble was on the damsel, for his voice was not the voice of Zurvan her betrothed; and she remembered the sorrow of Rukrooth. She would have fled from him, but a dread of the displeasure of the Chief restrained her, knowing Ruark a soul of wrath. Her eyelids dropped and the Chief gazed on her eagerly, and sang in a passion of praises of her; the fires of his love had a tongue, his speech was a torrent of flame at the feet of the damsel. And Bhanavar exclaimed, 'Oh, what am I, what am I, who have slain my love, my lover!—that one should love me and call on me for love? My life is a long weeping for him! Death is my wooer!'

Ruark still pleaded with her, and she said in fair gentleness, 'Speak not of it now in the freshness of my grief! Other times and seasons are there. My soul is but newly widowed!'

Fierce was the eye of the Chief, and he sprang up, crying, 'By the life of my head, I know thy wiles and the reading of these delays: but I'll never leave thee, nor lose sight of thee, Bhanavar! And think not to fly from me, thou subtle, brilliant Serpent! for thy track is my track, and thy condition my condition, and thy fate my fate. By Allah! this is so.'

Then he strode from her swiftly, and called to his Arabs. They had kindled a fire to roast the flesh of a buffalo, slaughtered by them from among a herd, and were laughing and singing beside the flames of the fire. So by the direction of their Chief the Arabs brought slices of sweet buffalo-flesh to Bhanavar, with cakes of grain: and Bhanavar ate alone, and drank from the waters before her. Then they laid for her a couch within the cave, and the aching of her spirit was lulled, and she slept there a dreamless sleep till morning.

By the morning light Bhanavar looked abroad for the Chief, and he was nowhere by. A pang of violent hope struck through her, and she pressed her bosom, praying he might have left her, and climbed the clefts and ledges of the mountain to search over the fair expanse of pasture beyond, for a trace of him departing. The sun was on the heads of the heavy flowers, and a flood of gold down the gorges, and a delicate rose hue on the distant peaks and upper dells of snow, which were as a crown to the scene she surveyed; but no sight of Ruark had she. And now she was beginning to rejoice, but on a sudden her eye caught far to east a glimpse of something in motion across an even slope of the lower hills leaning to the valley; and it was a herd that rushed forward, like a black torrent of the mountains flinging foam this way and that, and after the herd and at the sides of the herd she distinguished the white cloaks and scarfs and glittering steel of the Arabs of Ruark. Presently she saw a horseman break from the rest, and race in a line toward her. She knew this one for Ruark, and sighed and descended slowly to meet him. The greeting of the Chief was sharp, his manner wild, and he said little ere he said, 'I will see thee under the light of the Jewel, so tie it in a band and set it on thy brow, Bhanavar!'

Her mouth was open to intercede with his desire, but his forehead became black as night, and he shouted in the thunder of his lion-voice, 'Do this!'

She took the Jewel from its warm bed in her bosom, and held it, and got together a band of green weeds, and set it in the middle of the band, and tied the band on her brow, and lifted her countenance to the Chief. Ruark stood back from her and gazed on her; and he would have veiled his sight from her, but his hand fell. Then the might of her loveliness seized Bhanavar likewise, and the full orbs of her eyes glowed on the Chief as on a mirror, and she moved her serpent figure scornfully, and smiled, saying, 'Is it well?'

And he, when he could speak, replied, "Tis well! I have seen thee! for now can I die this day, if it be that I am to die. And well it is! for now know I there is truly no place but the tomb can hold me from thee!'

Bhanavar put the Jewel from her brow into her bosom, and questioned him, 'What is thy dread this day, O my Chief?'

He answered her gravely, 'I have seen Rukrooth my mother while I slept; and she was weeping, weeping by a stream, yea, a stream of blood; and it was a stream that flowed in a hundred gushes from her own veins. The sun of this dawn now, seest thou not? 'tis overcrimson; the vulture hangeth low down yonder valley.' And he cried to her, 'Haste! mount with me; for I have told Rukrooth a thing; and I know that woman crafty in the thwarting of schemes; such a fox is she where aught accordeth not with her forecastings, and the judgment of her love for me! By Allah! 'twere well we clash not; for that I will do I do, and that she will do doth she.'

So the twain mounted their steeds, and Ruark gathered his Arabs and placed them, some in advance, some on either side of Bhanavar; and they rode forward to the head of the valley, and across the meadows, through the blushing crowds of flowers, baths of freshest scents, cool breezes that awoke in the nostrils of the mares neighings of delight; and these pranced and curvetted and swung their tails, and gave expression to their joy in many graceful fashions; but a gloom was on Ruark, and a quick fire in his falcon-eye, and he rode with heels alert on the flanks of his mare, dashing onward to right and left, as do they that beat the jungle for the crouching tiger. Once, when he was well-nigh half a league in front, he wheeled his mare, and raced back full on Bhanavar, grasping her bridle, and hissing between his teeth, 'Not a soul shall have thee save I: by the tomb of my fathers, never, while life is with us!'

And he taunted her with bitter names, and was as one in the madness of intoxication, drunken with the aspect of her matchless beauty and with exceeding love for her. And Bhanavar knew that the dread of a mishap was on the mind of the Chief.

Now, the space of pasture was behind them a broad lake of gold and jasper, and they entered a region of hills, heights, and fastnesses, robed in forests that rose in rounded swells of leafage, each over each—above all points of snow that were as flickering silver flames in the farthest blue. This was the country of Bhanavar, and she gazed mournfully on the glades of golden green and the glens of iron blackness, and the wild flowers, wild blossoms, and weeds well known to her that would not let her memory rest, and were wistful of what had been. And she thought, 'My sisters tend the flocks, my mother spinneth with the maidens of the tribe, my father hunteth; how shall I come among them but strange? Coldly will they regard me; I shall feel them shudder when they take me to their bosoms.'

She looked on Ruark to speak with him, but the mouth of the Chief was set and white; and even while she looked, cries of treason and battle arose from the Arabs that were ahead, hidden by a branching wind of the way round a mountain slant. Then the eyes of the Chief reddened, his nostrils grew wide, and the darkness of his face was as flame mixed with smoke, and he seized Bhanavar and hastened onward, and lo! yonder were his men overmatched, and warriors of the mountains bursting on them from an ambush on all sides. Ruark leapt in his seat, and the light of combat was on him, and he dug his knees into his mare, and shouted the war-cry of his tribe, lifting his hands as it were to draw down wrath from the very heavens, and rushed to the encounter. Says the poet:

```
Hast thou seen the wild herd by the jungle galloping close?
With a thunder of hooves they trample what heads may oppose:
Terribly, crushingly, tempest-like, onward they sweep:
But a spring from the reeds, and the panther is sprawling in air,
And with muzzle to dust and black beards foam-lash'd, here and there,
Scatter'd they fly, crimson-eyed, track'd with blood to the deep.
```

Such was the onset of Ruark, his stroke the stroke of death; and ere the echoes had ceased rolling from that cry of his, the mountain-warriors were scattered before him on the narrow way, hurled down the scrub of the mountain, even as dead leaves and loosened stones; so like an arm of lightning was the Chief!

Now Ruark pursued them, and was lost to Bhanavar round a slope of the mountain. She quickened her pace to mark him in the glory of the battle, and behold! a sudden darkness enveloped her, and she felt herself in the swathe of tightened folds, clasped in an arm, and borne rapidly she knew not whither, for she could hear and see nothing. It was to her as were she speeding constantly downward in darkness to the lower realms of the Genii of the Caucasus, and every sense, and even that of fear, was stunned in her. How long an interval had elapsed she knew not, when the folds were unwound; but it was light of day, and the faces of men, and they were warriors that were about her, warriors of the mountain; but of Ruark and his Arabs no voice. So she said to them, 'What do ye with me?'

And one among them, that was a youth of dignity and grace, and a countenance like morning on the mountains, answered, 'The will of Rukrooth, O lady! and it is the plight of him we bow to with Rukrooth, mother of the Desert-Chief.'

She cried, 'Is he here, the Prince, that I may speak with him?'

The same young warrior made answer, 'Not so; forewarned was he, and well for him!'

Bhanavar drew her robe about her and was mute. Ere the setting of the moon they journeyed on with her; and continued so three days and nights through the defiles and ravines and matted growths of the mountains. On the fourth dawn they were on the summit of a lofty mountain-rise;

below them the sun, shooting a current of gold across leagues of sea. Then he that had spoken with Bhanavar said, 'A sail will come,' and a sail came from under the sun. Scarce had the ship grated shore when the warriors lifted Bhanavar, and waded through the water with her, and placed her unwetted in the ship, and one, the fair youth among the warriors, sprang on board with her, remaining by her. So the captain pushed off, and the wind filled the sails, and Bhanavar was borne over the lustre of the sea, that was as a changing opal in its lustre, even as a melted jewel flowing from the fingers of the maker, the Almighty One. The ship ceased not sailing till they came to a narrow strait, where the sea was but a river between fair sloping hills alight with towers and palaces, opening a way to a great city that was in its radiance over the waters of the sea as the aspect of myriad sheeny white doves breasting the wave. Hitherto the young warrior had held aloof in coldness of courtesy from Bhanavar; but now he sat by her, and said, 'The bond between my prince and Rukrooth is accomplished, and it was to snatch thee from the Chief of the Beni-Asser and bring thee even to this city.'

Bhanavar exclaimed, 'Allah be praised in all things, and his will be done!'

The youth continued, 'Thou art alone here, O lady, exposed to the perils of loneliness; surely it were well if I linger with thee awhile, and see to thy welfare in this city, even as a brother with a sister; and I will deal honourably by thee.'

Bhanavar looked on the young warrior and blushed at his exceeding sweetness with her; the soft freshness of his voice was to her as the blossom-laden breeze in the valleys of the mountains, and she breathed low the words of her gratitude, saying, 'If I am not a burden, let this be so.'

Then said he, 'Know me by my name, which is Almeryl; and that we seem indeed of one kin, make known unto me thine.'

She replied, 'Ill-omened is it, this name of Bhanavar!'

The youth among warriors gazed on her a moment with the fluttering eye of bashfulness, and said, 'Can they that have marked thee call thee other than Bhanavar the Beautiful?'

She remembered that Ruark had spoken in like manner, and the curse of her beauty smote her, and she thought, 'This fair youth, he hath not a mother to watch over him and ward off souls of evil. I dread there will come a mishap to him through me; Allah shield him from it!' And she sought to dissuade him from resting by her, but he cried, "Tis but a choice to dwell with thee or with the dogs in the street outside thy door, O Bhanavar!'

Now, the ship sailed close up to the quay, and cast anchor there in the midst of other ships of merchandise. Almeryl then threw a robe over his mountain dress and spoke with the captain apart, and he and Bhanavar took leave of the captain, and landed on the quay among the porters, and of these one stepped forward to them and shouted cheerily, 'Where be the burdens and the bales, O ye, fair couple fashioned in the eye of elegant proportions? Ye twin palm-trees, male and female! Wullahy! broad is the back of your servant.'

Almeryl beckoned to him that he should follow them, and he followed them, blessing the wind that had brought them to that city and the day. So they passed through the streets and lanes of the city, and the porter pointed out this house and that house wanting an occupant, and Almeryl fixed on one in an open thoroughfare that had before it a grass-plot, and behind a garden with fountains and flowers, and grass-knolls shaded by trees; and he paid down the half of its price, and had it furnished before nightfall sumptuously, and women in it to wait on Bhanavar, and stuffs and goods, and scents for the bath,—all luxuries whatsoever that tradesmen and merchants there could give in exchange for gold. Then Almeryl dismissed the porter in Allah's name, and gladdened his spirit with a gift over the due of his hire that exalted him in the eyes of the porter, and the porter went from him, exclaiming, 'In extremity Ukleet is thy slave!' and he sang:

> Shouldst thou see a slim youth with a damsel arriving,
> Be sure 'tis the hour when thy fortune is thriving;
> A generous fee makes the members so supple
> That over the world they could carry this couple.

Now so it was that the youth Almeryl and the damsel Bhanavar abode in the city they had come to weeks and months, and life to either of them as the flowing of a gentle stream, even as brother and sister lived they, chastely, and with temperate feasting. Surely the youth loved her with a great love, and the heart of Bhanavar turned not from him, and was won utterly by his gentleness and nobleness and devotion; and they relied on each other's presence for any joy, and were desolate in absence, as the poet says:

> When we must part, love,
> Such is my smart, love,
> Sweetness is savourless,
> Fairness is favourless!
> But when in sight, love,
> We two unite, love,
> Earth has no sour to me;
> Life is a flower to me!

And with the increase of every day their passion increased, and the revealing light in their eyes brightened and was humid, as is sung by him that luted to the rage of hearts:

> Evens star yonder
>   Comes like a crown on us,
> Larger and fonder
>   Grows its orb down on us;
> So, love, my love for thee
>   Blossoms increasingly;
> So sinks it in the sea,
>   Waxing unceasingly.

On a night, when the singing-girls had left them, the youth could contain himself no more, and caught the two hands of Bhanavar in his, saying, 'This that is in my soul for thee thou knowest, O Bhanavar! and 'tis spoken when I move and when I breathe, O my loved one! Tell me then the cause of thy shunning me whenever I would speak of it, and be plain with thee.'

For a moment Bhanavar sought to release herself from his hold, but the love in his eyes entangled her soul as in a net, and she sank forward to him, and sighed under his chin, "Twas indeed my very love of thee that made me.'

The twain embraced and kissed a long kiss, and leaned sideways together, and Bhanavar said, 'Hear me, what I am.'

Then she related the story of the Serpent and the Jewel, and of the death of her betrothed. When it was ended, Almeryl cried, 'And was this all?—this that severed us?' And he said, 'Hear what I am.'

So he told Bhanavar how Rukrooth, the mother of Ruark, had sent messengers to the Prince his father, warning him of the passage of Ruark through the mountains with one a Queen of Serpents, a sorceress, that had bewitched him and enthralled him in a mighty love for her, to the ruin of Ruark; and how the Chief was on his way with her to demand her in marriage at the hands of her parents; and the words of Rukrooth were, 'By the service that was between thee and my husband, and by the death he died, O Prince, rescue the Chief my son from this damsel, and entrap her from him, and have her sent even to the city of the inland sea, for no less a distance than that keepeth Ruark from her.'

And Almeryl continued, 'I questioned the messengers myself, and they told me the marvel of thy loveliness and the peril to him that looked on it, so I swore there was no power should keep me from a sight of thee, O my loved one! my prize! my life! my sleek antelope of the hills! Surely when my father appointed the warriors to lie in wait for thy coming, I slipped among them, so that they thought it ordered by him I should head them. The rest is known to thee, O my fountain of blissfulness! but the treachery to Ruark was the treachery of Ebn Asrac, not of such warriors as we; and I would have fallen on Ebn Asrac, had not Ruark so routed that man without faith. 'Twas all as I have said, blessed be Allah and his decrees!'

Bhanavar gazed on her beloved, and the bridal dew overflowed her underlids, and she loosed her hair to let it flow, part over her shoulders, part over his, and in sighs that were the measure of music she sang:

```
    I thought not to love again!
      But now I love as I loved not before;
    I love not; I adore!
 O my beloved, kiss, kiss me! waste thy kisses like a rain.
    Are not thy red lips fain?
      Oh, and so softly they greet!
      Am I not sweet?
    Sweet must I be for thee, or sweet in vain:
      Sweet to thee only, my dear love!
    The lamps and censers sink, but cannot cheat
      These eyes of thine that shoot above
      Trembling lustres of the dove!
    A darkness drowns all lustres: still I see
      Thee, my love, thee!
    Thee, my glory of gold, from head to feet!
 Oh, how the lids of the world close quite when our lips meet!
```

Almeryl strained her to him, and responded:

> My life was midnight on the mountain side;
>   Cold stars were on the heights:
> There, in my darkness, I had lived and died,
>   Content with nameless lights.
> Sudden I saw the heavens flush with a beam,
>   And I ascended soon,
> And evermore over mankind supreme,
>   Stood silver in the moon.

And he fell playfully into a new metre, singing:

> Who will paint my beloved
>   In musical word or colour?
> Earth with an envy is moved:
>   Sea-shells and roses she brings,
>   Gems from the green ocean-springs,
>   Fruits with the fairy bloom-dews,
>   Feathers of Paradise hues,
>   Waters with jewel-bright falls,
>   Ore from the Genii-halls:
> All in their splendour approved;
> All; but, match'd with my beloved,
>   Darker, and denser, and duller.

Then she kissed him for that song, and sang:

> Once to be beautiful was my pride,
>   And I blush'd in love with my own bright brow:
> Once, when a wooer was by my side,
>   I worshipp'd the object that had his vow:
> Different, different, different now,
>   Different now is my beauty to me:
> Different, different, different now!
>   For I prize it alone because prized by thee.

Almeryl stretched his arm to the lattice, and drew it open, letting in the soft night wind, and the sound of the fountain and the bulbul and the beam of the stars, and versed to her in the languor of deep love:

> Whether we die or we live,
>   Matters it now no more:
> Life has nought further to give:
>   Love is its crown and its core.
> Come to us either, we're rife,—
>   Death or life!
>
> Death can take not away,
>   Darkness and light are the same:
> We are beyond the pale ray,
>   Wrapt in a rosier flame:
> Welcome which will to our breath;
>   Life or death!

So did these two lovers lute and sing in the stillness of the night, pouring into each other's ears melodies from the new sea of fancy and feeling that flowed through them.

Ere they ceased their sweet interchange of tenderness, which was but one speech from one soul, a glow of light ran up the sky, and the edge of a cloud was fired; and in the blooming of dawn Almeryl hung over Bhanavar, and his heart ached to see the freshness of her wondrous loveliness; and he sang, looking on her:

```
The rose is living in her cheeks,
  The lily in her rounded chin;
She speaks but when her whole soul speaks,
  And then the two flow out and in,
And mix their red and white to make
  The hue for which I'd Paradise forsake.

Her brow from her black falling hair
  Ascends like morn: her nose is clear
As morning hills, and finely fair
  With pearly nostrils curving near
The red bow of her upper lip;
  Her bosom's the white wave beneath the ship.

The fair full earth, the enraptured skies,
  She images in constant play:
Night and the stars are in her eyes,
  But her sweet face is beaming day,
A bounteous interblush of flowers:
  A dewy brilliance in a dale of bowers.
```

Then he said, 'And this morning shall our contract of marriage be written and witnessed?'

She answered, 'As my lord willeth; I am his.'

Said he, 'And it is thy desire?'

She nestled to him and dinted his bare arm with the pearls of her mouth for a reply.

So that morning their contract of marriage was written, and witnessed by the legal number of witnesses in the presence of the Cadi, with his license on it endorsed; and Bhanavar was the bride of Almeryl, he her husband. Never was youth blessed in a bride like that youth!

Now, the twain lived together the circle of a full year of delightful marriage, and love lessened not in them, but was as the love of the first day. Little cared they, having each other, for the loneliness of their dwelling in that city, where they knew none save the porter Ukleet, who went about their commissions. Sometimes to amuse themselves with his drolleries, they sent for him, and were bountiful with him, and made him drink with them on the lawn of their garden leaning to an inlet of the sea; and then he would entertain them with all the scandal and gossip of the city, and its little folk and great. When he was outrageously extravagant in these stories of his, Bhanavar exclaimed, 'Are such things, now? can it be true?'

And he nodded in his conceit, and replied loftily, "Tis certain, O my Prince and Princess! ye be from the mountains, unused to the follies and dissipations of men where they herd; and ye know them not, men!'

The lamps being lit in the garden to the edges of the water, where they lay one evening, Ukleet, who had been in his briskest mood, became grave, and put his forefinger to the side of his nose and began, 'Hear ye aught of the great tidings? Wullahy! no other than the departure of the wife of Boolp, the broker, into darkness. 'Tis of Boolp ye hire this house, and had ye a hundred houses in this city ye might have had them from Boolp the broker, he that's rich; and glory to them whom Allah prospereth, say I! And I mention this matter, for 'tis certain now Boolp will take another wife to him to comfort him, for there be two things beloved of Boolp, and therein manifesteth he taste and the discernment of excellence, and what is approved; and of these two things let the love of his hoards of the yellow-skinned treasure go first, and after that attachment to the silver-skinned of creation, the fair, the rapturous; even to them! So by this see ye not Boolp will yearn in his soul for another spouse? Now, O ye well-matched pair! what a chance were this, knew ye but a damsel of the mountains, exquisite in symmetry, a moon to enrapture the imagination of Boolp, and in the nature of things herit his possessions! for Boolp is an old man, even very old.'

They laughed, and cried, 'We know not of such a damsel, and the broker must go unmarried for us.'

When next Ukleet sat before them, Almeryl took occasion to speak of Boolp again, and said, 'This broker, O Ukleet, is he also a lender of money?'

Ukleet replied, 'O my Prince, he is or he is not: 'tis of the maybes. I wot truly Boolp is one that baiteth the hook of an emergency.'

The brows of the Prince were downcast, and he said no more; but on the following morning he left Bhanavar early under a pretext, and sallied forth from the house of their abode alone.

Since their union in that city they had not been once apart, and Bhanavar grieved and thought, 'Waneth his love for me?' and she called her women to her, and dressed in this dress and that dress, and was satisfied with none. The dews of the bath stood cold upon her, and she trembled, and fled from mirror to mirror, and in each she was the same surpassing vision of loveliness. Then her women held a glass to her, and she examined herself closely, if there might be a fleck upon her anywhere, and all was as the snow of the mountains on her round limbs sloping in the curves of harmony, and the faint rose of the dawn on slants of snow was their hue. Twining her fingers and sighing, she thought, 'It is not that! he cannot but think me beautiful.' She smiled a melancholy smile at her image in the glass, exclaiming, 'What availeth it, thy beauty? for he is away and looketh not on thee, thou vain thing! And what of thy loveliness if the light illumine it not, for he is the light to thee, and it is darkness when he's away.'

Suddenly she thought, 'What's that which needeth to light it no other light? I had well-nigh forgotten it in my bliss, the Jewel!' Then she went to a case of ebony-wood, where she kept the Jewel, and drew it forth, and shone in the beam of a pleasant imagination, thinking, "Twill surprise him!' And she robed herself in a robe of saffron, and set lesser gems of the diamond and the emerald in the braid of her hair, and knotted the Serpent Jewel firmly in a band of gold-threaded tissue, and had it woven in her hair among the braids. In this array she awaited his coming, and pleased her mind with picturing his astonishment and the joy that would be his. Mute were the women who waited on her, for in their lives they had seen no such sight as Bhanavar beneath the beams of the Jewel, and the whole chamber was aglow with her.

Now, in her anxiety she sent them one and one repeatedly to look forth at the window for the coming of the Prince. So, when he came not she went herself to look forth, and stretched her white neck beyond the casement. While her head was exposed, she heard a cry of some one from the house in the street opposite, and Bhanavar beheld in the house of the broker an old wrinkled fellow that gesticulated to her in a frenzy. She snatched her veil down and drew in her head in anger at him, calling to her maids, 'What is yonder hideous old dotard?'

And they answered, laughing, ''Tis indeed Boolp the broker, O fair mistress and mighty!'

To divert herself she made them tell her of Boolp, and they told her a thousand anecdotes of the broker, and verses of him, and the constancy of his amorous condition, and his greediness. And Bhanavar was beguiled of her impatience till it was evening, and the Prince returned to her. So they embraced, and she greeted him as usual, waiting what he would say, searching his countenance for a token of wonderment; but the youth knew not that aught was added to her beauty, for he looked nowhere save in her eyes. Bhanavar was nigh weeping with vexation, and pushed him from her, and chid him with lack of love and weariness of her; and the eye of the Prince rose to her brow to read it, and he saw the Jewel. Almeryl clapped his hands, crying, 'Wondrous! And this thy surprise for me, my fond one? beloved of mine!' Then he gazed on her a space, and said, 'Knowest thou, thou art terrible in thy beauty, Bhanavar, and hast the face of lightning under that Jewel of the Serpent?'

She kissed him, whispering, 'Not lightning to thee! Yet lovest thou Bhanavar?'

He replied, 'Surely so; and all save Bhanavar in this world is the darkness of oblivion to me.'

When it was the next morning, Almeryl rose to go forth again. Ere he had passed the curtain of the chamber Bhanavar caught him by the arm, and she was trembling violently. Her visage was a wild inquiry: 'Thou goest?—and again? There is something hidden from me!'

Almeryl took her to his heart, and caressed her with fond flatteries, saying, 'Ask but what is beating under these two pomegranates, and thou learnest all of me.'

But she stamped her foot, crying, 'No! no! I will hear it! There's a mystery.'

So he said, 'Well, then, it is this only; small matter enough. I have a business with the captain of the vessel that brought us hither, and I must see him ere he setteth sail; no other than that, thou jealous, watchful star! Pierce me with thine eyes; it is no other than that.'

She levelled her lids at him till her lustrous black eyelashes were as arrows, and mimicked him softly, 'No other than that?'

And he replied, 'Even so.'

Then she clung to him like a hungry creature, repeating, 'Even so,' and let him go. Alone, she summoned a slave, a black, and bade him fetch to her without delay Ukleet the porter, and the porter was presently ushered in to her, protesting service and devotion. So, she questioned him of Almeryl, and the Prince's business abroad, what he knew of it. Ukleet commenced reciting verses on the ills of jealousy, but Bhanavar checked him with an eye that Ukleet had seen never before in woman or in man, and he gaped at her helplessly, as one that has swallowed a bone. She laughed, crying, 'Learn, O thou fellow, to answer my like by the letter.'

Now, what she heard from Ukleet when he had recovered his wits, was that the Prince had a business with none save the lenders of money. So she spake to Ukleet in a kindly tone, 'Thou art mine, to serve me?'

He was as one fascinated, and delivered himself, 'Yea, O my mistress! with tongue-service, toe-service, back-service, brain-service, whatso pleaseth thy sweet presence.'

Said she, 'Hie over to the broker opposite, and bring him hither to me.'

Ukleet departed, saying, 'To hear is to obey.'

She sat gazing on the Jewel and its counterchanging splendours in her hand, and the thought of Almeryl and his necessity was her only thought. Not ten minutes of the hour had passed before the women waiting on her announced Ukleet and the broker Boolp. Bhanavar gave little heed to the old fellow's grimaces, and the compliments he addressed her, but handed him the Jewel and desired his valuation of its worth. The face of Boolp was a keen edge when he regarded Bhanavar, but the sight of the Jewel sharpened it tenfold, and he tossed his arms, exclaiming, 'A jewel, this!'

So Bhanavar cried to him, 'Fix a price for it, O thou broker!'

And Boolp, the old miser, debated, and began prating,

'O lady! the soul of thy slave is abashed by a double beam, this the jewel of jewels, thou truly of thy sex; and saving thee there's no jewel of worth like this one, and together ye be—wullahy! never felt I aught like this since my espousal of Soolka that 's gone, and 'twas nothing like it then! Now, O my Princess, confess it freely—this is but a pretext, this valuation of the Jewel, and Ukleet our go-between; and leave the rewarding of him to me. Wullahy! I can be generous, and my days of favour with fair ladies be not yet over. Blessed be Allah for this day! And thinkest thou those eyes fell on me with discriminating observation ere my sense of perception was struck by thee? Not so, for I had noted thee, O moon of hearts, from my window yonder.'

In this fashion Boolp the broker went on prating, and bowing, and screwing the corners of his little acid eyes to wink the wink of common accord between himself and Bhanavar. Meantime she had spoken aside to one of her women, and a second black slave entered the chamber, bearing in his hand a twisted scourge, and that slave laid it on the back of Boolp the broker, and by this means he was brought quickly to the valuation of the Jewel. Then he named a sum that was a great sum, but not the value of the Jewel to the fiftieth part, nay nor the five-hundredth part, of its value; and Ukleet remonstrated with him, but he was resolute, saying, 'Even that sum leaves me a beggar.'

So Bhanavar said, 'My desire is for immediate payment of the money, and the Jewel is thine for that sum.'

Now the broker went to fetch the money, and returned with it in bags of gold one-half the amount, and bags of silver one-third, and the remainder in writing made due at a certain period for payment. And he groaned and handed her the money, and took the Jewel in his hands; ejaculating, 'In the name of Allah!'

That evening, when it was dark and the lamps lit in the chamber, and the wine set and the nosegay, Almeryl asked of Bhanavar to see her under the light of the Jewel. She warded him with an excuse, but he was earnest with her. So she feigned that he teased her, saying, "Tis that thou art no longer content with me as I am, O my husband!' Then she said, 'Wert thou successful in thy dealings this day?'

His arm slackened round her, and he answered nothing. So she cried, 'Fie on thee, thou foolish one! and what is thy need of running over this city? Know I not thy case and thine occasion, O my beloved? Surely I am Queen of Serpents, a mistress of enchantments, a diviner of things hidden, and I know thee. Here, then, is what thou requirest, and conceal not from me thy necessity another time, my husband!'

Upon that she pointed his eye to the money-bags of gold and of silver. Almeryl was amazed, and asked her, 'How came these? for I was at the last extremity, without coin of any kind.'

She answered, 'How, but by the Serpents!'

And he exclaimed, 'Would that I might work as that porter worketh, rather than this!'

Now, seeing he bewailed her use of the powers of the Jewel, Bhanavar fell between his arms, and related to him her discovery of his condition, and how she disposed of the Jewel to the broker, and of the scourging of Boolp; and he praised her, and clave to her, and they laughed and delighted their souls in plenteousness, and bliss was their portion; as the poet says,

```
Bliss that is born of mutual esteem
And tried companionship, I truly deem
A well-based palace, wherein fountains rise
From springs that have their sources in the skies.
```

So were they for awhile. It happened that one day, that was the last day of the year since her wearing of the Jewel, Ukleet said to them, 'Be wary! the Vizier Aswarak hath his eye on you, and it is no cool one. I say nothing: the wise are discreet in their tellings of the great. 'Tis certain the broker Boolp forgetteth not his treatment here.'

They smiled, turning to each other, and said, 'We live innocently, we harm no one, what should we fear?'

During the night of that day Bhanavar awoke and kissed the Prince; and lo! he shuddered in his sleep as with the grave-cold. A second time she was awakened on the breast of Almeryl by a dream of the Serpents of the Lake Karatis—the lake of the Jewel; and she stood up, and there was in the street a hum of voices, and she saw there before the house armed men with naked steel in their hands. Scarce had she called Almeryl to her, when the outer door of their house was forced, and she shrieked to him, ''Tis thou they come for: fly, O my Prince, my husband! the way of the garden is clear.'

But he said sadly, 'Nay, what am I? it is thou they would win from me. I'll leave thee not in this life.'

So she cried, 'O my soul, then together!—but I shall hinder thee, and be a burden to thy flight.'

And she called on the All-powerful for aid, and ran with him into the garden of the house, and lo! by the water side at the end of the garden a boat full of armed soldiers with scimitars. So these fell upon them, and bound them, and haled them into the house again, where was the dark Vizier Aswarak, and certain officers of the night watch with a force. The Vizier cried when he saw them, 'I accuse thee, Prince Almeryl, of being here in the city of our lord the King, to conspire against him and his authority.'

Almeryl faced the Vizier firmly, and replied, 'I knew not in my life I had made an enemy; but there is one here who telleth that of me.'

The Vizier frowned, saying, 'Thou deniest this? And thou here, and thy father at war with the sovereignty of our lord the King!'

Almeryl beheld his danger, and he said, 'Is this so?'

Then cried the Vizier, 'Hear him! is not that a fair simulation?' So he called to the guard, 'Shackle him!' When that was done, he ordered the house to be sacked, and the women and the slaves he divided for a spoil, but he reserved Bhanavar to himself: and lo! twice she burst away from them that held her to hang upon the lips of Almeryl, and twice was she torn from him as a grape-bunch is torn from the streaming vine, and the third time she swooned and the anguish of life left her.

Now, Bhanavar was borne to the harem of the Vizier, and for days she suffered no morsel of food to enter her mouth, and was dying, had not the Vizier in the cunning of his dissimulation fed her with distant glimpses of Almeryl, to show her he yet lived. Then she thought, 'While my beloved liveth, life is due to me'; and she ate and drank and reassumed her fair fulness and the queenliness that was hers; but the Vizier had no love of her, and respected her, considering in his mind, 'Time will exhaust the fury of this tigress, and she is a fruit worth the waiting for. Wullahy! I shall have possessed her ere the days of over-ripening.'

There was in the harem of the Vizier a mountain-girl that had been brought there in her childhood, and trained to play upon the lute and accompany her voice with the instrument. To this little damsel Bhanavar gave her heart, and would listen all day, as in a trance, to her luting, till the desire to escape from that bondage and gather tidings of Almeryl mastered her, and she persuaded one of the blacks of the harem with a bribe to procure her an interview with the porter Ukleet. So at a certain hour of the night Ukleet was introduced into the garden of the harem, and he was in the darkness of that garden a white-faced porter with knees that knocked the dread-march together; but Bhanavar strengthened his soul, and he said to her, "Twas the doing of Boolp the broker: and he whispered the Vizier of thee and thy beauty, O my mistress! Surely thy punishment and this ruin is but part payment to Boolp of the price of the Jewel, the great Jewel that's in the hands of the Vizier.'

Then she questioned him: 'And Almeryl, the Prince, my husband, what of him?'

Ukleet was dumb, and Bhanavar asked to hear no more. Surely she was at the gates of pale spirits within an hour of her interview with Ukleet, and there was no blessedness for her save in death, the stiffer of ills, the drug that is infallible. As is said:

```
Dark is that last stage of sorrow
Which from Death alone can borrow
Comfort:—
```

Bhanavar would have died then, but in a certain pause of her fever the Vizier stood by her. She looked at him long as she lay, and the life in her large eyes was ebbing away slowly; but there seemed presently a check, as an eddy comes in the stream, and the light of intelligence flowed like a reviving fire into her eyes, and her heart quickened with desire of life while she looked on the Vizier. So she passed the pitch of that fever, and bloomed anew in her beauty, and cherished it, for she had a purpose.

Now, there was rejoicing in the harem of the Vizier Aswarak when Bhanavar arose from the couch; and the Vizier exulted, thinking, 'I have tamed this wild beauty, or she had reached death in that extremity.' So he allowed Bhanavar greater freedom and indulgences, and Bhanavar feigned to give her soul to the pleasures women delight in, and the Vizier buried her in gems and trinkets and costly raiment, robes of exquisite silks, the choicest of Samarcand and China; and he permitted her to make purchases among certain of the warehouses of the city and the shops of the tradesmen, jewellers and others, so that she went about as she would, but for the slaves that attended her and the overseer of the harem. This continued, and Aswarak became urgent with her, and to remove suspicion from him she named a day from that period when she would be his. Meantime she contrived to see Ukleet the porter frequently, and within a week of her engagement with the Vizier she gazed from a lattice-window of the harem, and beheld in the garden, by the beams of the moon, Ukleet, and he was looking as on the watch for her. So she sent to him the little mountain-girl she loved, but Ukleet would tell her nothing; then went she herself, greeting him graciously, for his service was other than that of self-seeking.

Ukleet said, 'O Lady, mistress of hearts, moon of the tides of will! 'tis certain I was thy slave from the hour I beheld thee first, and of the Prince, thy husband; Allah rest his soul! Now these be my tidings. Wullahy! the King is one maddened with the reports I've spread about of thy beauty, yea! raging. And I have a friend in his palace, even an under-cook, acute in the interpreting of wishes. There was he always gabbling of thy case, O my Princess, till the head-cook seized hold on it, and so it went to the chamberlain, thence to the chief of the eunuchs, and from him in a natural course, to the King. Now from the King the tracking of this tale went to the under-cook down again, and from him to me. So was I summoned to the King, and the King discoursed with me—I with him, in fair fluency; he in ejaculations of desire to have sight of thee, I in expatiation on that he would see when he had his desire. Now in this have I not done thee a service, O sovereign of fancies?'

Bhanavar mused and said, 'On the after-morrow I pass through the city to make a selection of goods, and I shall pass at noon by the great mosque, on my way to the shop of Ebn Roulchook, the King's jeweller, beyond the meat-market. Of a surety, I know not how my lord the King may see me.'

Said the porter, "Tis enough! on my head be it.' And he went from her, singing the song:

```
How little a thing serves Fortune's turn
  When she's intent on doing!
How easily the world may burn
  When kings come out a-wooing!
```

Now, ere she set forth on the after-morrow to make her purchases, Bhanavar sent word to the Vizier Aswarak that she would see him, and he came to her drunken with alacrity, for he augured favourably that her reluctance was melting toward him: so she said, 'O my master, my time of mourning is at an end, and I would look well before thee, even as one worthy of being thy bride; so bestow on me, I pray thee, for my wearing that day, the jewels that be in thy treasury, the brightest and clearest of them, and the largest.'

The Vizier Aswarak replied, and he was one in great satisfaction of soul, 'All that I have are thine. Wullahy! and one, a marvel, that I bought of Boolp the broker, that had it from an African merchant.' So he commanded the box wherein he had deposited the Jewel to be brought to him there in the chamber of Bhanavar, and took forth the Serpent Jewel between his forefinger and thumb, and laughed at the eager eyes of Bhanavar when she beheld it, saying, "Tis thine! thy bridal gift the day I possess thee.'

Bhanavar trembled at the sight of the Jewel, and its redness was to her as the blood of Zurvan and Almeryl. She stretched her hand out for it and cried, 'This day, O my lord, make it mine.'

So the Vizier said, 'Nay, what I have spoken will I keep to; it has cost me much.'

Bhanavar looked at him, and uttered in a soft tone, 'Truly it has cost thee much.'

Then she exclaimed, as in play, 'See me, how I look by its beam.' And in her guile she snatched the Jewel from him, and held it to her brow. Then Aswarak started from her and feared her, for the red light of the Jewel glowed, and darkened the chamber with its beam, darkening all save the lustre that was on the visage of Bhanavar. He shouted, 'What's this! Art thou a sorceress?'

She removed the Jewel, and ceased glaring on him, and said, 'Nothing but thy poor slave!'

Then he coaxed her to give him the Jewel, and she would not; he commanded her peremptorily, and she hesitated; so he grasped her tightened hand, and his face loured with wrath; yet she withheld the Jewel from him laughing; and he was stirred to extreme wrath, and drew from his girdle the naked scimitar, and menaced her with it. And he looked mighty; but she dreaded him little, and stood her full height before him, daring him, and she was as the tigress defending a cub from a wilder beast. Now when he was about to call in the armed slaves of the palace, she said, 'I warn thee, Vizier Aswarak! tempt me not to match them that serve me with them that serve thee.'

He ground his teeth in fury, crying, 'A conspiracy! and in the harem! Now, thou traitress! the logic of the lash shall be tried upon thee.' And he roared, 'Ho! ye without there! ho!'

But ere the slaves had entered Bhanavar rubbed the Jewel on her bosom, muttering, 'I have forborne till now! Now will I have a sacrifice, though I be it.' And rubbing the Jewel, she sang,

```
Hither! hither!
  Come to your Queen;
Come through the grey wall,
  Come through the green!
```

There was heard a noise like the noise of a wind coming down a narrow gorge above falling waters, a hissing and a rushing of wings, and behold! Bhanavar was circled by rings and rings of serpent-folds that glowed round her, twisted each in each, with the fierceness of fire, she like a flame rising up white in the midst of them. The black slaves, when they had lifted the curtain of the harem-chamber, shrieked to see her, and Aswarak crouched at her feet with the aspect of an angry beast carved in stone. Then Bhanavar loosed on either of the slaves a serpent, saying, 'What these have seen they shall not say.' And while the sweat dropped heavily from the forehead of Aswarak, she stepped out of the circle of serpents, singing,

```
Over! over!
  Hie to the lake!
Sleep with the left eye,
  Keep the right awake.
```

Then the serpents spread with a great whirr, and flew through the high window and the walls as they had come, and she said to the Vizier, 'What now? Fearest thou? I have spared thee, thou that madest me desolate! and thy slaves are a sacrifice for thee. Now this I ask: Where lies my beloved, the Prince my husband? Speak nothing of him, save the place of his burial!'

So he told her, 'In the burial-ground of the great prison.'

She rolled her eyes on the Vizier darkly, exclaiming, 'Even where the felons lie entombed, he lieth!' And she began to pant, pale with what she had done, and leaned to the floor, and called,

```
    Yellow stripe, with freckle red,
    Coil and curl, and watch by my head.
```

And a serpent with yellow stripes and red freckles came like a javelin down to her, and coiled and curled round her head, and she slept an hour. When she arose the Vizier was yet there, sitting with folded knees. So she sped the serpent to the Lake Karatis, and called her women to her, and went to an inner room, and drew an outer robe and a vest over that she had on, and passed the Vizier, and said, 'Art thou not rejoiced in thy bride, O Aswarak? 'Twas a wondrous clemency, hers! Now but four more days and thou claimest her. Say nothing of what thou hast seen, or thou wilt shortly see nothing further to say, my master.'

So she left the Vizier sitting still in that chamber, and mounted a mule, attended by slaves on foot before and behind her, and passed through the streets till she came to the shop of Ebn Roulchook. The King was in disguise at the extremity of the shop, and while she examined this and that of the precious stones, Bhanavar for a moment made bare the beauty, of her face, and love's fires took fast hold of the King, and he cried, 'I marvel not at the eloquence of the porter.'

Now, she made Ebn Roulchook bring to her a circlet of gold, with a hollow in the frontal centre, and fit into that hollow the Serpent Jewel. So, while she laughed and chatted with her women Bhanavar lifted the circlet, and made her countenance wholly bare even to the neck and the beginning slope of the bosom, and fixed the circlet to her head with the Jewel burning on her brow. Then when he beheld the glory of excelling loveliness that she was, and the splendour in her eyes under the Jewel, the King shouted and parted with his disguise, and Ebn Roulchook and the women and slaves with Bhanavar fled to the courtyard that was behind the shop, leaving Bhanavar alone with the King. Surely Bhanavar returned not to the dwelling of the Vizier.

Now, the King Mashalleed espoused Bhanavar, and she became his queen and ruled him, and her word was the dictate of the land. Then caused she the body of Almeryl, with the severed head of the Prince, to be disinterred, and entombed secretly in the palace; and she had lamps lit in the vault, and the pall spread, and the readers of the Koran to read by the tomb; and then she stole to the tomb hourly, in the day and in the night, wailing of him and her utter misery, repeating verses at the side of the tomb, and they were,

```
        Take me to thee!
      Like the deep-rooted tree,
    My life is half in earth, and draws
    Thence all sweetness; oh may my being pause
        Soon beside thee!

        Welcome me soon!
      As to the queenly moon,
    Man's homage to my beauty sets;
    Yet am I a rose-shrub budding regrets:
        Welcome me soon.

        Soul of my soul!
      Have me not half, but whole.
    Dear dust, thou art my eyes, my breath!
    Draw me to thee down the dark sea of death,
        Soul of my soul!
```

And she sang:

```
      Sad are they who drink life's cup
        Till they have come to the bitter-sweet:
      Better at once to toss it up,
        And trample it beneath the feet;
      For venom-charged as serpents' eggs
        'Tis then, and knows not other change.
      Early, early, early, have I reached the dregs
   Of life, and loathe and love the bittersweet, revenge!
```

Then turned she aside, and sang musingly:

```
      I came to his arms like the flower of the spring,
      And he was my bird of the radiant wing:
      He flutter'd above me a moment, and won
      The bliss of my breast as a beam of the sun,
      Untouch'd and untasted till then—
```

The voice in her throat was like a drowning creature, and she rose up, and chanted wildly:

```
         I weep again?

   What play is this? for the thing is dead in me long since:
   Will all the reviving rain
   Of heaven bring me back my Prince?
   But I, when I weep, when I weep,
      Blood will I weep!
   And when I weep,
   Sons for fathers shall weep;
   Mothers for sons shall weep;
   Wives for husbands shall weep!
   Earth shall complain of floods red and deep,
      When I weep!
```

Upon that she ran up a secret passage to her chamber and rubbed the Jewel, and called the serpents, to delight her soul with the sight of her power, and rolled and sported madly among them, clutching them by the necks till their thin little red tongues hung out, and their eyes were as discoloured blisters of venom. Then she arose, and her arms and neck and lips were glazed with the slime of the serpents, and she flung off her robes to the close-fitting silken inner vest looped across her bosom with pearls, and whirled in a mazy dance-measure among them, and sang melancholy melodies, making them delirious, fascinating them; and they followed her round and round, in twines and twists and curves, with arched heads and stiffened tails; and the chamber swam like an undulating sea of shifting sapphire lit by the moon of midnight. Not before the moon of midnight was in the sky ceased Bhanavar sporting with the serpents, and she sank to sleep exhausted in their midst.

Such was the occupation of the Queen of Mashalleed when he came not to her. The women and slaves of the palace dreaded her, and the King himself was her very slave.

Meanwhile the plot of her unforgivingness against Aswarak ripened: and the Vizier beholding the bride he had lost Queen of Mashalleed his master, it was as she conceived, that his heart was eaten with jealousy and fierce rage. Bhanavar as she came across him spake mildly, and gave him gentle looks, sad glances, suffering not his fires to abate, the torment of his love to cool. Each night he awoke with a serpent in his bed; the beam of her beauty was as the constant bite of a serpent, poisoning his blood, and he deluded his soul with the belief that Bhanavar loved him notwithstanding, and that she was seized forcibly from him by the King. 'Otherwise,' thought he, 'why loosed she not a serpent from the host to strangle me even as yonder black slaves?' Bhanavar knew the mind of Aswarak, and considered, 'The King is cunning and weak, a slave to his desires, and in the bondage of the jewel, my beauty. The Vizier is unscrupulous, a hatcher of intrigues; but that he dreads me and hopes a favour of me, he would have wrought against me ere now. 'Tis then a combat 'twixt him and me. O my soul, art thou dreaming of a fair youth that was the bliss of thy bosom night and day, night and day? The Vizier shall die!'

One morning, and it was a year from the day she had become Queen of Mashalleed, Bhanavar sprang up quickly from the side of the King; and he was gazing on her in amazement and loathing. She flew to her chamber, chasing forth her women, and ran to a mirror. Therein she saw three lines that were on her brow, lines of age, and at the corners of her mouth and about her throat a slackness of skin, the skin no longer its soft rosy white, but withered brown as leaves of the forest. She shrieked, and fell back in a swoon of horror. When she recovered, she ran to the mirror again, and it was the same sight. And she rose from swooning a third time, and still she beheld the visage of a hag; nothing of beauty there save the hair and the brilliant eyes. Then summoned she the serpents in a circle, and the number of them was that of the days in the year: and she bared her wrist and seized one, a gray-silver with sapphire spots, and hissed at him till he hissed, and foam whitened the lips of each. Thereupon she cried:

```
Treble-tongue and throat of hell,
What is come upon me, tell!
```

And the Serpent replied,

```
Jewel Queen! beauty's price!
'Tis the time for sacrifice!
```

She grasped another, one of leaden colour, with yellow bars and silver crescents, and cried:

```
Treble-tongue and throat of fire,
Name the creature ye require!
```

And the Serpent replied:

```
Ruby lip! poison tooth!
We are hungry for a youth.
```

She grasped another that writhed in her fingers like liquid emerald, and cried:

```
Treble-tongue and throat of glue!
How to know the one that's due?
```

And the Serpent replied:

>     Breast of snow! baleful bliss!
>     He that wooing wins a kiss.

She clutched one at her elbow, a hairy serpent with yellow languid eyes in flame-sockets and livid-lustrous length—a disease to look on, and cried:

>     Treble-tongue and throat of gall!
>     There's a youth beneath the pall.

And the Serpent replied:

>     Brilliant eye! bloody tear!
>     He has fed us for a year.

She squeezed that hairy serpent till her finger-points whitened in his neck, and he dropped lifelessly, crying:

>     Treble-tongues and things of mud!
>     Sprang my beauty from his blood?

And the Serpents rose erect, replying:

>     Yearly one of us must die;
>      Yearly for us dieth one;
>     Else the Queen an ugly lie
>      Lives till all our lives be done!

Bhanavar stood up, and hurried them to Karatis. When she was alone she fell toward the floor, repeating, "Tis the Curse!' Suddenly she thought, 'Yet another year my beauty shall be nourished by my vengeance, yet another! And, O Vizier, the kiss shall be thine, the kiss of doom; for I have doomed thee ere now. Thou, thou shalt restore me to my beauty: that only love I now my Prince is lost.'

So she veiled her face in the close veil of the virtuous, and despatched Ukleet, whom she exalted in the palace of the King, to the Vizier; and Ukleet stood before Aswarak, and said, 'O Vizier, my mistress truly is longing for you with excessive longing, and in what she now undergoeth is forgotten an evil done by you to her; and she bids you come and concert with her a scheme deliberately as to the getting rid of this tyrant who is an affliction to her, and her life is lessened by him.'

The Vizier was deceived by his passion, and he chuckled and exclaimed, 'My very dream! and to mind me of her, then, she sent the serpents! Wullahy, in the matter of women, wait! For, as the poet declareth:

>     'Tis vanity our souls for such to vex;
>     Patience is a harvest of the sex.''

And they fret themselves not overlong for husbands that are gone, these young beauties. I know them. Tell the Queen of Serpents I am even hers to the sole of my foot.'

So it was understood between them that the Vizier should be at the gate of the garden of the palace that night, disguised; and the Vizier rejoiced, thinking, 'If she have not the Jewel with her, it shall go ill with me, and I foiled this time!'

Ukleet then proceeded to the house of Boolp the broker, fronting the gutted ruins where Bhanavar had been happy in her innocence with Almeryl, the mountain prince, her husband. Boolp was engaged haggling with a slave-merchant the price of a fair slave, and Ukleet said to him,'Yet awhile delay, O Boolp, ere you expend a fraction of treasure, for truly a mighty bargain of jewels is waiting for you at the palace of my lord the King. So come thither with all your money-bags of gold and silver, and your securities, and your bonds and dues in writing, for 'tis the favourite of the King requireth you to complete a bargain with her, and the price of her jewels is the price of a kingdom.'

Said Boolp, 'Hearing is compliance in such a case.'

And Ukleet continued, 'What a fortune is yours, O Boolp! truly the tide of fortune setteth into your lap. Fail not, wullahy! to come with all you possess, or if you have not enough when she requireth it to complete the bargain, my mistress will break off with you. I know not if she intend even other game for you, O lucky one!'

Boolp hitched his girdle and shrugged, saying, "Tis she will fail, I wot,—she, in having therewith to complete the bargain between us. Wa! wa!—there! I've done this before now. Wullahy! if she have not enough of her rubies and pearls to outweigh me and my gold, go to, Boolp will school her! What says the poet?—

```
''Earth and ocean search, East, West, and North, to the South,
  None will match the bright rubies and pearls of her mouth.''
```

'Aha! what? O Ukleet! And he says:

```
   ''The lovely ones a bargain made
    With me, and I renounced my trade,
   Half-ruined; 'Ah!' said they, 'return and win!
   To even scales ourselves we will throw in!'''
```

How so? But let discreetness reign and security flourisheth!'

Ukleet nodded at him, and repeated the distich:

```
   Men of worth and men of wits
   Shoot with two arrows, and make two hits.
```

So he arranged with Boolp the same appointment as with the Vizier, and returned to Queen Bhanavar.

Now, in the dark of night Aswarak stood within the gate of the palace-garden of Mashalleed that was ajar, and a hand from a veiled figure reached to him, and he caught it, in the fulness of his delusion, crying, 'Thou, my Queen?' But the hand signified silence, and drew him past the tank of the garden and through a court of the palace into a passage lit with lamps, and on into a close-curtained chamber, and beyond a heavy curtain into another, a circular passage descending between black hangings, and at the bottom a square vault draped with black, and in it precious woods burning, oils in censers, and the odour of ambergris and myrrh and musk floating in clouds, and the sight of the Vizier was for a time obscured by the thickness of the incenses floating. As he became familiar with the place, he saw marked therein a board spread at one end with viands and wines, and the nosegay in a water-vase, and cups of gold and a service of gold,—every preparation for feasting mightily. So the soul of Aswarak leapt, and he cried, 'Now unveil thyself, O moon of our meeting, my mistress!'

The voice of Bhanavar answered him, 'Not till we have feasted and drunken, and it seemeth little in our eyes. Surely the chamber is secure: could I have chosen one better for our meeting, O Aswarak?'

Upon that he entreated her to sit with him to the feast, but she cried, 'Nay! delay till the other is come.'

Cried he, 'Another?'

But she exclaimed, 'Hush!' and saying thus went forward to the foot of the passage, and Boolp was there, following Ukleet, both of them under a weight of bags and boxes. So she welcomed the broker, and led him to the feast, he coughing and wheezing and blinking, unwitting the vexation of the Vizier, nor that one other than himself was there. When Boolp heard the voice of the Vizier, in astonishment, addressing him, he started back and fell upon his bags, and the task of coaxing him to the board was as that of haling a distempered beast to the water. Then they sat and feasted together, and Ukleet with them; and if Aswarak or Boolp waxed impatient of each other's presence, he whispered to them, 'Only wait! see what she reserveth for you.' And Bhanavar mused with herself, 'Truly that reserved shall be not long coming!' So they drank, and wine got the mastery of Aswarak, so that he made no secret of his passion, and began to lean to her and verse extemporaneously in her ear; and she stinted not in her replies, answering to his urgency in girlish guise, sighing behind the veil, as if under love's influence. And the Vizier pressed close, and sang:

```
'Tis said that love brings beauty to the cheeks
  Of them that love and meet, but mine are pale;
For merciless disdain on me she wreaks,
  And hides her visage from my passionate tale:
I have her only, only when she speaks.
      Bhanavar, unveil!

I have thee, and I have thee not! Like one
  Lifted by spirits to a shining dale
In Paradise, who seeks to leap and run
  And clasp the beauty, but his foot doth fail,
For he is blind: ah! then more woful none!
      Bhanavar, unveil!
```

He thrust the wine-cup to her, and she lifted it under her veil, and then sang, in answer to him:

>     My beauty! for thy worth
>         Thank the Vizier!
>
>     He gives thee second birth:
>         Thank the Vizier!
>
>     His blooming form without a fault:
>         Thank the Vizier!
>
>     Is at thy foot in this blest vault:
>         Thank the Vizier!
>
>     He knoweth not he telleth such a truth,
>         Thank the Vizier!
>
>     That thou, thro' him, spring'st fresh in blushing youth:
>         Thank the Vizier!
>
>     He knoweth little now, but he shall soon be wise:
>         Thank the Vizier!
>
>     This meeting bringeth bloom to cheeks and lips and eyes:
>         Thank the Vizier!
>
>     O my beloved in this blest vault, if I love thee for aye,
>         Thank the Vizier!
>
>     Thine am I, thine! and learns his soul what it has taught—to die,
>         Thank the Vizier!

Now, Aswarak divined not her meaning, and was enraptured with her, and cried, 'Wullahy! so and such thy love! Thine am I, thine! And what a music is thy voice, O my mistress! 'Twere a bliss to Eblis in his torment could he hear it. Life of my head! and is thy beauty increased by me? Nay, thou flatterer!' Then he said to her, 'Away with these importunate dogs! 'tis the very hour of tenderness! Wullahy! they offend my nostril: stung am I at the sight of them.'

She rejoined,—

>         O Aswarak! star of the morn!
>     Thou that wakenest my beauty from night and scorn,
>         Thy time is near, and when 'tis come,
>     Long will a jackal howl that this thy request had been dumb.
>         O Aswarak! star of the morn!

So the Vizier imaged in his mind the neglect of Mashalleed from these words, and said, 'Leave the King to my care, O Queen of Serpents, and expend no portion of thy power on him; but hasten now the going of these fellows; my heart is straitened by them, and I, wullahy! would gladly see a serpent round the necks of either.'

She continued,—

> O Aswarak! star of the morn!
> Lo! the star must die when splendider light is born;
> In stronger floods the beam will drown:
> Shrink, thou puny orb, and dread to bring me my crown,
> O Aswarak! star of the morn!

Then said she, 'Hark awhile at those two! There's a disputation between them.'

So they hearkened, and Ukleet was pledging Boolp, and passing the cup to him; but a sullenness had seized the broker, and he refused it, and Ukleet shouted, 'Out, boon-fellow! and what a company art thou, that thou refusest the pledge of friendliness? Plague on all sulkers!'

And the broker, the old miser, obstinate as are the half-fuddled, began to mumble, 'I came not here to drink, O Ukleet, but to make a bargain; and my bags be here, and I like not yonder veil, nor the presence of yonder Vizier, nor the secresy of this. Now, by the Prophet and that interdict of his, I'll drink no further.'

And Ukleet said, 'Let her not mark your want of fellowship, or 'twill go ill with you. Here be fine wines, spirited wines! choice flavours! and you drink not! Where's the soul in you, O Boolp, and where's the life in you, that you yield her to the Vizier utterly? Surely she waiteth a gallant sign from you, so challenge her cheerily.'

Quoth Boolp, 'I care not. Shall I leave my wealth and all I possess void of eyes? and she so that I recognise her not behind the veil?'

Ukleet pushed the old miser jeeringly: 'You not recognise her? Oh, Boolp, a pretty dissimulation! Pledge her now a cup to the snatching of the veil, and bethink you of a fitting verse, a seemly compliment,—something sugary.'

Then Boolp smoothed his head, and was bothered; and tapped it, and commenced repeating to Bhanavar:

> I saw the moon behind a cloud,
> And I was cold as one that's in his shroud:
> And I cried, Moon!—

Ukleet chorused him, 'Moon!' and Boolp was deranged in what he had to say, and gasped,—

> Moon! I cried, Moon!—and I cried, Moon!

Then the Vizier and Ukleet laughed till they fell on their backs; so Bhanavar took up his verse where he left it, singing,—

> And to the cry
> Moon did make fair the following reply:
> 'Dotard, be still! for thy desire
> Is to embrace consuming fire.'

Then said Boolp, 'O my mistress, the laws of conviviality have till now restrained me; but my coming here was on business, and with me my bags, in good faith. So let us transact this matter of the jewels, and after that the song of—

```
''Thou and I
A cup will try,''
```

even as thou wilt.'

Bhanavar threw aside her outer robe and veil, and appeared in a dress of sumptuous blue, spotted with gold bees; her face veiled with a veil of gauzy silver, and she was as the moon in summer heavens, and strode mar jestically forward, saying, 'The jewels? 'tis but one. Behold!'

The lamps were extinguished, and in her hand was the glory of the Serpent Jewel, no other light save it in the vaulted chamber.

So the old miser perked his chin and brows, and cried wondering, 'I know it, this Jewel, O my mistress.'

She turned to the Vizier, and said, lifting the red gloom of the Jewel on him, 'And thou?'

Aswarak ate his under-lip.

Then she cried, 'There's much ye know in common, ye two.'

Thereupon Bhanavar passed from the feast on to the centre of the vault, and stood before the tomb of Almeryl, and drew the cloth from it; and they saw by the glow of the Jewel that it was a tomb. When she had mounted some steps at the side of the tomb, she beckoned them to come, crying, in a voice of sobs, 'This which is here, likewise ye may know.'

So they came with the coldness of a mystery in their blood, and looked as she looked intently over a tomb. The lid was of glass, and through the glass of the lid the Jewel flung a dark rosy ray on the body of Almeryl lying beneath it.

Now, the miser was perplexed at the sight; but Aswarak stepped backward in defiance, bellowing, ''Twas for this I was tricked to come here! Is 't fooling me a second time? By Allah! look to it; not a second time will Aswarak be fooled.'

Then she ran to him, and exclaimed, 'Fooled? For what cam'st thou to me?'

And he, foaming and grinding his breath, 'Thou woman of wiles! thou serpent! but I'll be gone from here.'

So she faltered in sweetness, knowing him doomed, and loving to dally with him in her wickedness, 'Indeed if thou cam'st not for my kiss—'

Then said the Vizier, 'Yet a further guile! Was't not an outrage to bring me here?'

She faltered again, leaning the fair length of her limbs on a couch, "Tis ill that we are not alone, else could these lips convince thee well: else indeed!'

And the Vizier cried, 'Chase then these intruders from us, O thou sorceress, and above all serpents in power! for thou poisonest with a touch; and the eye and the ear alike take in thy poisons greedily. Thou overcomest the senses, the reason, the judgment; yea, vindictiveness, wrath, suspicions; leading the soul captive with a breath of thine, as 'twere a breeze from the gardens of bliss.'

Bhanavar changed her manner a little, lisping, 'And why that starting from the tomb of a dead harmless youth? And that abuse of me?'

He peered at her inquiringly, echoing 'Why?'

And she repeated, as a child might repeat it, 'Why that?'

Then the Vizier smote his forehead in the madness of utter perplexity, changing his eye from Bhanavar to the tomb of Almeryl, doubting her truth, yet dreading to disbelieve it. So she saw him fast enmeshed in her subtleties, and clapped her hands crying, 'Come again with me to the tomb, and note if there be aught I am to blame in, O Aswarak, and plight thyself to me beside it.'

He did nothing save to widen his eye at her somewhat; and she said, 'The two are yonside the tomb, and they hear us not, and see us not by this light of the Jewel; so come up to it boldly with me; free thy mind of its doubt, and for a reconcilement kiss me on the way.'

Aswarak moved not forward; but as Bhanavar laid the Jewel in her bosom he tore the veil from her darkened head, and caught her to him and kissed her. Then Bhanavar laughed and shouted, 'How is it with thee, Vizier Aswarak?'

He was tottering, and muttered, "Tis a death-chill hath struck me even to my marrow.'

So she drew the Jewel forth once more, and rubbed it ablaze, and the noise of the Serpents neared; and they streamed into the vault and under it in fiery jets, surrounding Bhanavar, and whizzing about her till in their velocity they were indivisible; and she stood as a fountain of fire clothed in flashes of the underworld, the new loveliness of her face growing vivid violet like an incessant lightning above them. Then stretched she her two hands, and sang to the Serpents:—

```
Hither, hither, to the feast!
Hither to the sacrifice!
Virtue for my sake hath ceased:
Now to make an end of Vice!

Twisted-tail and treble-tongue,
Swelling length and greedy maw!
I have had a horrid wrong;
Retribution is the law!

Ye that suck'd my youthful lord,
```

```
            Now shall make another meal:
            Seize the black Vizier abhorr'd;
            Seize him! seize him throat and heel!

            Set your serpent wits to find
            Tortures of a new device:
            Have him! have him heart and mind!
            Hither to the sacrifice'
```

Then she whirled with them round and round as a tempest whirls; and when she had wound them to a fury, lo, she burst from the hissing circle and dragged Ukleet from the vault into the passage, and blocked the entrance to the vault. So was Queen Bhanavar avenged.

Now, she said to Ukleet, 'Ransom presently the broker,—him they will not harm,' and hastened to the King that he might see her in her beauty. The King reclined on cushions in the harem with a fair slave-girl, newly from the mountains, toying with the pearls in her locks. Then thought Bhanavar, 'Let him not slight me!' So she drew a rose-coloured veil over her face and sat beside Mashalleed. The King continued his fondling with the girl, saying to her, 'Was there no destiny foretold of thy coming to the palace of the King to rule it, O Nashta, starbeam in the waters! and hadst thou no dream of it?'

Bhanavar struck the King's arm, but he noticed her not, and Nashta laughed. Then Bhanavar controlled her trembling and said, 'A word, O King! and vouchsafe me a hearing.'

The King replied languidly, still looking on Nashta, "Tis a command that the voice of none that are crabbed and hideous be heard in the harem, and I find comfort in it, O Nashta! but speak thou, my fountain of sweet-dropping lute-notes!'

Bhanavar caught the King's hand and said, 'I have to speak with thee; 'tis the Queen. Chase from us this little wax puppet a space.'

The King disengaged his hand and leaned it over to Nashta, who began playing with it, and fitting on it a ring, giggling. Then, as he answered nothing, Bhanavar came nearer and slapped him on the cheek. Mashalleed started to his feet, and his hand grasped his girdle; but that wrathfulness was stayed when he beheld the veil slide from her visage. So he cried, 'My Queen! my soul!'

She pointed to Nashta, and the King chid the girl, and sent her forth lean with his shifted displeasure, as a kitten slinks wet from a fish-pond where it had thought to catch a great fish. Then Bhanavar exclaimed, 'There was a change in thy manner to me before that creature.'

He sought to dissimulate with her, but at last he confessed, 'I was truly this morning the victim of a sorcery.'

Thereupon she cried, 'And thou went angered to find me not by thee on the couch, but one in my place, a hag of ugliness. Hear then the case, O Mashalleed! Surely that old crone had a dream, and it was that if she slept one night by the King she would arise fresh in health from her ills, and with powers lasting a year to heal others of all maladies with a touch. So she came to me, petitioning me to bring this about. O my lord the King, did I well in being privy to her desire?'

The King could not doubt this story of Bhanavar, seeing her constant loveliness, and the arch of her flashing brow, and the oval of her cheek and chin smooth as milk. So he said, 'O my Queen! I had thought to go, as I must, gladly; but how shall I go, knowing thy truth, thy beauty unchanged; thee faithful, a follower of the injunctions of the Prophet in charitable deeds?'

Cried she, 'And whither goeth my lord, and on what errand?'

He answered, 'The people of a province southward have raised the standard of revolt and mocked my authority; they have been joined by certain of the Arab chiefs subject to my dominion, and have defeated my armies. 'Tis to subdue them I go; yea, to crush them. Yet, wallaby! I know not. Care I if kingdoms fall away, and nations, so that I have thee? Nay, let all pass, so that thou remain by me.'

Bhanavar paced from him to a mirror, and frowned at the reflection of her fairness, thinking, 'Such had he spoken to the girl Nashta, or another, this King!' And she thought, 'I have been beloved by the noblest three on earth; I will ask no more of love; vengeance I have had. 'Tis time that I demand of my beauty nothing save power, and I will make this King my stepping-stone to power, rejoicing my soul with the shock of armies.'

Now, she persuaded Mashalleed to take her with him on his expedition against the Arabs; and they set forth, heading a great assemblage of warriors, southward to the land bordering the Desert. The King credited the suggestions of Bhanavar, that Aswarak had disappeared to join the rebels, and pressed forward in his eagerness to inflict a chastisement signal in swiftness upon them and that traitor; so eagerly Mashalleed journeyed to his army in advance, that the main body, with Bhanavar, was left by him long behind. She had encouraged him, saying, 'I shall love thee much if thou art speedy in winning success.' The Queen was housed on an elephant, harnessed with gold, and with silken purple trappings; from the rose-hued curtains of her palanquin she looked on a mighty march of warriors, filling the extent of the plains; all day she fed her sight on them. Surely the story of her beauty became noised among the guards of her person that rode and ran beneath the royal elephant, till the soldiers of Mashalleed spake but of the beauty of the Queen, and Bhanavar was as a moon shining over that sea of men.

Now, they had passed the cultivated fields, and were halting by the ford of a river bordering the Desert, when lo! a warrior on the yonside, riding in a cloud of dust, and his shout was, 'The King Mashalleed is defeated, and flying.' Then the Captains of the host witnessed to the greatness of Allah, and were troubled with a dread, fearing to advance; but Bhanavar commanded a horse to be saddled for her, and mounted it, and plunged through the ford singly; so they followed her, and all day she rode forward on horseback, touching neither food nor drink. By night she was a league beyond the foremost of them, and fell upon the King encamped in the Desert, with the loose remnant of his forces. Mashalleed, when he had looked on her, forgot his affliction, and stood up to embrace her, but Bhanavar spurned him, crying, 'A time for this in the time of disgrace?' Then she said, 'How came it?'

He answered, 'There was a Chief among the enemy, an Arab, before the terror of whom my people fled.'

Cried she, 'Conquer him on the morrow, and till then I eat not, drink not, sleep not.'

On the morrow Mashalleed again encountered the rebels, and Bhanavar, seated on her elephant, from a sand-hillock under a palm, beheld the prowess of the Arab Chief and the tempest of battle that he was. She thought, 'I have seen but one mighty in combat like that one, Ruark, the Chief of the Beni-Asser.' Thereupon she coursed toward the King, even where the arrows gloomed like locusts, thick and dark in the air aloof, and said, 'The victory is with yonder Chief! Hurl on him three of thy sons of valour.'

The three were selected, and made onslaught on this Chief, and perished under his arm.

Bhanavar saw them fall, and exclaimed, 'Another attack on him, and with thrice three!'

Her will was the mandate of Mashalleed, and these likewise were ordered forth, and closed on the Chief, but he darted from their toils and wheeled about them, spearing them one by one till the nine were in the dust. Bhanavar compressed her dry lips and muttered to the King, 'Head thou a body against him.'

Mashalleed gathered round his standard the chosen of his warriors, and smoothed his beard, and headed them. Then the Chief struck his lance behind him, and stretched rapidly a half-circle across the sand, and halted on a knoll. When they neared him he retreated in a further half-circle, and continued this wise, wasting the fury of Mashalleed, till he stood among his followers. There, as the King hesitated and prepared to retreat, he and the others of the tribe levelled their lances and hung upon his rear, fretting them, slaughtering captains of the troop. When Mashalleed turned to face his pursuer, the Chief was alone, immovable on his mare, fronting the ranks. Then Bhanavar taunted the King, and he essayed the capture of that Chief a second time and a third, and it was each time as the first. Bhanavar looked about her with rapid eyes, murmuring, 'Oh, what a Chief is he! Oh that a cloud would fall, a smoke arise, to blind these hosts, that I might sling my serpents on him unseen, for I will not be vanquished, though it be by Ruark!' So she drew to the King, and the altercation between them was fierce in the fury of the battle, he saying, ''Tis a feint of the Chief, this challenge; and I must succour the left of my army by the well, that he is overmatching with numbers'; and she, 'If thou head them not, then will I, and thou shalt behold a woman do what thou durst not, and lose her love and win her scorn.' While they spake the Arabs they looked on seemed to flutter and waver, and the Chief was backing to them, calling to them as 'twere words of shame to rally them. Seeing this, Mashalleed charged against the Chief once more, and lo! the Arabs opened to receive him, closing on his band of warriors like waters whitened by the storm on a fleet of swift-scudding vessels: and there was a dust and a tumult visible, such as is seen in the darkness when a vessel struck by the lightning-bolt is sinking—flashes of steel, lifting of hands, rolling of horsemen and horses. Then Bhanavar groaned aloud, 'They are lost! Shame to us! only one hope is left-that 'tis Ruark, this Chief!' Now, the view of the plain cleared, and with it she beheld the army of Mashalleed broken, the King borne down by a dust of Arabs; so she unveiled her face and rode on the host with the horsemen that guarded her, glorious with a crown of gold and the glowing Jewel on her brow. When she was a javelin's flight from them the Arabs shouted and paused in terror, for the light of her head was as the sun setting between clouds of thunder; but that Chief dashed forward like a flame beaten level by the wind, crying, 'Bhanavar; Bhanavar!' and she knew the features of Ruark; so she said, 'Even I!' And he cried again, 'Bhanavar! Bhanavar!' and was as one stricken by a shaft. Then Bhanavar threw on him certain of the horsemen with her, and he suffered them without a sign to surround him and grasp his mare by the bridle-rein, and bring him, disarmed, before the Queen. At sight of Ruark a captive the Arabs fell into confusion, and lost heart, and were speedily chased and scattered from the scene like a loose spray before the wind; but Mashalleed the King rejoiced mightily and praised Bhanavar, and the whole army of the King praised her, magnifying her.

Now, with Ruark she interchanged no syllable, and said not farewell to him when she departed with Mashalleed, to encounter other tribes; and the Chief was bound and conducted a prisoner to the city of the inland sea, and cast into prison, in expectation of Death the releaser, and continued there wellnigh a year, eating the bitter bread of captivity. In the evening of every seventh day there came to him a little mountain girl, that sat by him and leaned a lute to her bosom, singing of the mountain and the desert, but he turned his face from her to the wall. One day she sang of Death the releaser, and Ruark thought, "Tis come! she warneth me! Merciful is Allah!' On the morning that followed Ukleet entered the cell, and with him three slaves, blacks, armed with scimitars. So Ruark stood up and bore witness to his faith, saying, 'Swift with the stroke!' but Ukleet exclaimed, 'Fear not! the end is not yet.'

Then said he, 'Peace with thee! These slaves, O Chief, excelling in martial qualities! surely they're my retinue, and the retinue of them of my rank in the palace; and where I go they go; for the exalted have more shadows than one! yea, three have they in my case, even very grimly black shadows, whereon the idle expend not laughter, and whoso joketh in their hearing, 'tis, wullahy! the last joke of that person. In such-wise are the powerful known among men, they that stand very prominent in the beams of prosperity! Now this of myself; but for thee—of a surety the Queen Bhanavar, my mistress, will be here by the time of the rising of the moon. In the name of Allah!' Saying that he departed in his greatness, and Ruark watched for her that rose in his soul as the moon in the heavens.

Meanwhile Bhanavar had mused, "Tis this day, the day when the Serpents desire their due, and the King Mashalleed they shall have; for what is life to him but a treachery and a dalliance, and what is my hold on him but this Jewel of the Serpents? He has had the profit of beauty, and he shall yield the penalty: my kiss is for him, my serpent-kiss. And I will release Ruark, and espouse him, and war with kings, sultans, emperors, infidels, subduing them till they worship me.'

She flashed her figure in the glass, and was lovely therein as one in the light of Paradise; but ere she reached the King Mashalleed, lo! the hour of the Serpents had struck, and her beauty melted from her as snow melts from off the rock; and she was suddenly haggard in utter uncomeliness, and knew it not, but marched, smiling a grand smile, on to the King. Now as Mashalleed lifted his eyes to her he started amazed, crying, 'The hag again!' and she said, 'What of the hag, O my lord the King?' Thereat he was yet more amazed, and exclaimed, 'The hag of ugliness with the voice of Bhanavar! Has then the Queen lent that loathsomeness her voice also?'

Bhanavar chilled a moment, and looked on the faces of the women present, and they were staring at her, the younger ones tittering, and among them Nashta, whom she hated. So she cried, 'Away with ye!' But the King commanded them, 'Stay!' Then the Queen leaned to him, saying, 'I will speak with my lord alone'; whereat he shrank from her, and spat. Ice and flame shivered through the blood of Bhanavar, yet such was her eagerness to give the kiss to Mashalleed, that she leaned to him, still wooing him to her with smiles. Then the King seized her violently, and flung her over the marble floor to the very basin of the fountain, and the crown that was on her brow fell and rolled to the feet of Nashta. The girl lifted it, laughing, and was in the act of fitting it to her fair head amid the chuckles of her companions, when a slap from the hand of Bhanavar spun her twice round, and she dropped to the marble insensible. The King bellowed in wrath, and ran to Nashta, crying to the Queen, 'Surrender that crown to her, foul hag!' But Bhanavar had bent over the basin of the fountain, and beheld the image of her change therein, and was hurrying from the hall and down the corridors of the palace to the private chamber. So he made bare the steel by his side, and followed her with a number of the harem guard, menacing her, and commanding her to surrender the crown with the Jewel. Ere she could lay hand on a veil, he was beside her, and she was encompassed. In that extremity Bhanavar plucked the Jewel from her crown, and rubbed it, calling the Serpents to her. One came, one only, and that one would not move from her to sling himself about the neck of Mashalleed, but whirled round her, hissing:

```
Every hour a serpent dies,
Till we have the sacrifice:
Sweeten, sweeten, with thy kiss,
Quick! a soul for Karatis.
```

Surely the King bit his breath, marvelling, and his fury became an awful fear, and he fell back from her, molesting her no further. Then she squeezed the serpent till his body writhed in knots, and veiled herself, and sprang down a secret passage to the garden, and it was the time of the rising of the moon. Coolness and soothingness dropped on her as a balm from the great light, and she gazed on it murmuring, as in a memory:

```
Shall I counsel the moon in her ascending?
Stay under that dark palm-tree through the night,
   Rest on the mountain slope,
   By the couching antelope,
O thou enthroned supremacy of light!
 And for ever the lustre thou art lending
Lean on the fair long brook that leaps and leaps,
   Silvery leaps and falls:
   Hang by the mountain-walls,
Moon! and arise no more to crown the steeps,
 For a danger and dolour is thy wending!
```

And she panted and sighed, and wept, crying, 'Who, who will kiss me or have my kiss now, that I may indeed be as yonder beam? Who, that I may be avenged on this King? And who sang that song of the ascending of the moon, that comes to me as a part of me from old times?' As she gazed on the circled radiance swimming under a plume of palm leaves, she exclaimed, 'Ruark! Ruark the Chief!' So she clasped her hands to her bosom, and crouched under the shadows of the garden, and fled through the garden gates and the streets of the city, heavily veiled, to the prison where Ruark awaited her within the walls and Ukleet without. The Governor of the prison had been warned by Ukleet of her coming, and the doors and bars opened before her unchallenged, till she stood in the cell of Ruark; her eyes, that were alone unveiled, scanned the countenance of the Chief, the fevered lustre-jet of his looks, and by the little moonlight in the cell she saw with a glance the straw-heap and the fetters, and the black-bread and water untasted on the bench—signs of his misery and desire for her coming. So she greeted him with the word of peace, and he replied with the name of the All-Merciful. Then said she, 'O Ruark, of Rukrooth thy mother tell me somewhat.'

He answered, 'I know nought of her since that day. Allah have her in his keeping!'

So she cried, 'How? What say'st thou, Ruark? 'tis a riddle.'

Then he, 'The oath of Ruark is no rope of sand! He swore to see her not till he had set eyes on Bhanavar.'

She knelt by the Chief, saying in a soft voice, 'Very greatly the Chief of the Beni-Asser loved Bhanavar.' And she thought, 'Yea! greatly and verily love I him; and he shall be no victim of the Serpents, for I defy them and give them other prey.' So she said in deeper notes, 'Ruark! the Queen is come hither to release thee. O my Chief! O thou soul of wrath! Ruark, my fire-eye! my eagle of the desert! where is one on earth beloved as thou art by Bhanavar?' The dark light in his eyes kindled as light in the eyes of a lion, and she continued, 'Ruark, what a yoke is hers who weareth this crown! He that is my lord, how am I mated to him save in loathing? O my Chief, my lion! hadst thou no dream of Bhanavar, that she would come hither to unbind thee and lift thee beside her, and live with thee in love and veilless loveliness,—thine? Yea! and in power over lands and nations and armies, lording the infidel, taming them to submission, exulting in defiance and assaults and victories and magnanimities—thou and she?' Then while his breast heaved like a broad wave, the Queen started to her feet, crying, 'Lo, she is here! and this she offereth thee, Ruark!'

A shrill cry parted from her lips, and to the clapping of her hands slaves entered the cell with lamps, and instruments to strike off the fetters from the Chief; and they released him, and Ruark leaned on their shoulders to bear the weight of a limb, so was he weakened by captivity; but Bhanavar thrust them from the Chief, and took the pressure of his elbow on her own shoulder, and walked with him thus to the door of the cell, he sighing as one in a dream that dreameth the bliss of bliss. Now they had gone three paces onward, and were in the light of many lamps, when behold! the veil of Bhanavar caught in the sleeve of Ruark as he lifted it, and her visage became bare. She shrieked, and caught up her two hands to her brow, but the slaves had a glimpse of her, and said among themselves, 'This is not the Queen.' And they murmured, ''Tis an impostor! one in league with the Chief.' Bhanavar heard them say, 'Arrest her with him at the Governor's gate,' and summoned her soul, thinking, 'He loveth me, the Chief! he will look into my eyes and mark not the change. What need I then to dread his scorn when I ask of him the kiss: now must it be given, or we are lost, both of us!' and she raised her head on Ruark, and said to him, 'my Chief, ere we leave these walls and join our fates, wilt thou plight thyself to me with a kiss?'

Ruark leapt to her like the bounding leopard, and gave her the kiss, as were it his whole soul he gave. Then in a moment Bhanavar felt the blush of beauty burn over her, and drew the veil down on her face, and suffered the slaves to arrest her with Ruark, and bring her before the Governor, and from the Governor to the King in his council-chamber, with the Chief of the Beni-Asser.

Now, the King Mashalleed called to her, 'Thou traitress! thou sorceress! thou serpent!'

And she answered under the veil, 'What, O my lord the King! and wherefore these evil names of me?'

Cried he, 'Thou thing of guile! and thou hast pleaded with me for the life of the Chief thus long to visit him in secret! Life of my head I but Mashalleed is not one to be fooled.'

So she said, "Tis Bhanavar! hast thou forgotten her?'

Then he waxed white with rage, exclaiming, 'Yea, 'tis she! a serpent in the slough! and Ukleet in the torture hath told of thee what is known to him. Unveil! unveil!'

She threw the veil from her figure, and smiled, for Mashalleed was mute, the torrent of invective frozen on his mouth when he beheld the miracle of beauty that she was, the splendid jewel of throbbing loveliness. So to scourge him with the bitter lash of jealousy, Bhanavar turned her eyes on Ruark, and said sweetly, 'Yet shalt thou live to taste again the bliss of the Desert. Pleasant was our time in it, O my Chief!' The King glared and choked, and she said again, 'Nor he conquered thee, but I; and I that conquered thee, little will it be for me to conquer him: his threats are the winds of idleness.'

Surely the world darkened before the eyes of Mashalleed, and he arose and called to his guard hoarsely, 'Have off their heads!' They hesitated, dreading the Queen, and he roared, 'Slay them!'

Bhanavar beheld the winking of the steel, but ere the scimitars descended, she seized Ruark, and they stood in a whizzing ring of serpents, the sound of whom was as the hum of a thousand wires struck by storm-winds. Then she glowed, towering over them with the Chief clasped to her, and crying:

```
King of vileness! match thy slaves
With my creatures of the caves.
```

And she sang to the Serpents:

```
Seize upon him! sting him thro'!
Thrice this day shall pay your due.
```

But they, instead of obeying her injunction, made narrower their circle round Bhanavar and the Chief. She yellowed, and took hold of the nearest Serpent horribly, crying:

```
Dare against me to rebel,
Ye, the bitter brood of hell?
```

And the Serpent gasped in reply:

> One the kiss to us secures:
> Give us ours, and we are yours.

Thereupon another of the Serpents swung on, the feet of Ruark, winding his length upward round the body of the Chief; so she tugged at that one, tearing it from him violently, and crying:

> Him ye shall not have, I swear!
> Seize the King that's crouching there.

And that Serpent hissed:

> This is he the kiss ensures:
> Give us ours, and we are yours.

Another and another Serpent she flung from the Chief, and they began to swarm venomously, answering her no more. Then Ruark bore witness to his faith, and folded his arms with the grave smile she had known in the desert; and Bhanavar struggled and tussled with the Serpents in fierceness, strangling and tossing them to right and left. 'Great is Allah!' cried all present, and the King trembled, for never was sight like that seen, the hall flashing with the Serpents, and a woman-serpent, their Queen, raging to save one from their fury, shrieking at intervals:

> Never, never shall ye fold,
> Save with me the man I hold.

But now the hiss and scream of the Serpents and the noise of their circling was quickened to a slurred savage sound and they closed on Ruark, and she felt him stifling and that they were relentless. So in the height of the tempest Bhanavar seized the Jewel in the gold circlet on her brow and cast it from her. Lo! the Serpents instantly abated their frenzy, and flew all of them to pluck the Jewel, chasing the one that had it in his fangs through the casement, and the hall breathed empty of them. Then in the silence that was, Bhanavar veiled her face and said to the Chief, 'Pass from the hall while they yet dread me. No longer am I Queen of Serpents.'

But he replied, 'Nay! said I not my soul is thine?'

She cried to him, 'Seest thou not the change in me? I was bound to those Serpents for my beauty, and 'tis gone! Now am I powerless, hateful to look on, O Ruark my Chief!'

He remained still, saying, 'What thou hast been thou art.'

She exclaimed, 'O true soul, the light is hateful to me as I to the light; but I will yet save thee to comfort Rukrooth, thy mother.'

So she drew him with her swiftly from the hall of the King ere the King had recovered his voice of command; but now the wrath of the All-powerful was upon her and him! Surely within an hour from the flight of the Serpents, the slaves and soldiers of Mashalleed laid at his feet two heads that were the heads of Ruark and Bhanavar; and they said, 'O great King, we tracked them to her chamber and through to a passage and a vault hung with black, wherein were two corpses, one in a tomb and one unburied, and we slew them there, clasping each other, O King of the age!'

Mashalleed gazed upon the head of Bhanavar and sighed, for death had made the head again fair with a wondrous beauty, a loveliness never before seen on earth.

END OF VOLUME-1

www.ingramcontent.com/pod-product-compliance
Lightning Source LLC
LaVergne TN
LVHW090039080526
838202LV00046B/3878